Threaded Needles

A NOVEL

Arianna Snow

Golden Horse Ltd.
Cedar Rapids, Iowa

This book is primarily a book of fiction. Names, characters, places and incidents are either products of the author's imagination or actual historic places and events which have been used fictitiously for historical reference as noted.

An *Original Publication of Golden Horse Ltd.*
P.O. Box 1002
Cedar Rapids, IA 52406-1002 U.S.A.

www.ariannaghnovels.com

ISBN 10: 0-9772308-3-X
ISBN 13: 9780977230839

Library of Congress Control Number: 2007940005

First Printing
Printed and bound in the United States of America
by Publishers' Graphics, LLC Carol Stream, IL

Cover: Design by Arianna Snow
        Photography by CEZ
        Layout by CEZ
        Printed by White Oak Printing, Lancaster PA

In Memory

of

Jack,

my dear Parrolet, of many years

and

Gesadt,

my friends' sweet Hannoverian

My gratitude and love to:

God,

my husband,

everything

KAE, CE, LC

editorial

my parents and husband

for bookkeeping and packaging

DA

word processing

family and **friends**

support

HIRAM GEOFFREY MCDONNALLY FAMILY TREE

PATERNAL GRANDPARENTS
CAPTAIN GEOFFREY EDWARD MCDONNALLY
CATHERINE NORTON MCDONNALLY

FATHER
CAPTAIN GEOFFREY LACHLAN MCDONNALLY

UNCLE
EDWARD CALEB MCDONNALLY

MATERNAL GRANDPARENTS
ALEXANDER THOMAS SELRACH
SARAH GLASGOW SELRACH

MOTHER
AMANDA SELRACH MCDONNALLY

SISTER
HANNAH RUTH MCDONNALLY

NIECE
SOPHIA MCDONNALLY

CARETAKERS
ALBERT ZIGMANN
ELOISE ZIGMANN

SON- GUILLAUME ZIGMANN

FRIENDS
DANIEL O'LEARDON
ABIGAIL O'LEARDON

NAOMI BEATRICE (MACKENZIE) MCDONNALLY FAMILY TREE

PATERNAL GRANDPARENTS
JEREMIAH NORMAN MACKENZIE
OCTAVIA HILL MACKENZIE

FATHER
NATHAN ELIAS MACKENZIE
DAGMAR ARNOLDSON MACKENZIE (STEPMOTHER)

MATERNAL GRANDPARENTS
JAMES HENRY SMITHFIELD
IRENE CLEBOURNE SMITHFIELD

MOTHER
BEATRICE SMITHFIELD MACKENZIE

BROTHER
JEREMIAH JAMES MACKENZIE

DAUGHTER
ALLISON SARAH O'CONNOR

HUSBAND
EDWARD CALEB MCDONNALLY

SISTER
NATALIA MACKENZIE

FRIENDS
HARRIET DUGAN
JOSEPH DUGAN

HENRY MCTAVISH

The Chapters

Chapter 1

"Delilah"

"The whole essence
of true gentle-breeding
lies in the wish
and the art
to be agreeable."

—Oliver Wendell Holmes

The inhabitants of the illustrious, sprawling mansion of Lochmoor Glen's, Brachney Hall spent the March evening of nineteen-hundred and fourteen engaged in a highly competitive game of pinochle. Master of the estate, Edward McDonnally, confined to a wheelchair with a broken arm and leg, paired up with his fiancée, Naomi, to challenge their worthy opponents. Sophia McDonnally and Daniel O'Leardon, Edward's great niece and his nephew Hiram's best friend, proved to be a powerful match.

"I do believe that your injuries are affecting your judgment, Uncle Edward," Sophia snickered.

"Nonsense, if anything, the disturbances from the library have impaired my talents," Edward defended.

"Aye, me sister and Hiram have been goin' at it for some time," Daniel agreed.

"Perhaps, having those two in such close quarters was unfavorable to our plan," Naomi suggested.

"The storm has past, I tell you. I witnessed the proposal. You will see," Sophia smiled.

Within a short time, Naomi and Edward's playing skills proved to be insufficient. The strategic talents of the shrewd Sophia and her insightful partner led them to certain victory, while the dueling couple in the adjacent room resolved their seemingly irreconcilable differences, as Sophia predicted.

During the past week, Hiram McDonnally discovered that having the position as one of the wealthiest men in Britain, topped off with being, allegedly, the most attractive, was ironically detrimental to developing his desired relationship with Miss O'Leardon. Although Hiram never flaunted his social status or displayed conceit, Abigail, of lower social standing, assumed that his designs on her were purely superficial and temporary, at most. However, as the evening progressed, Hiram's irresistible charm and their sincere confessions drew Hiram and Abigail into a *temporary* blissful union. Their subsequent conflict in personality transformed into a binding love, not at all hindered by their mutual physical attraction. After sharing their first kiss in the questionable privacy of the library, they went to meet with the other guests. The grins of the card players in the drawing room were notable proof to the conspiracy of their matchmaking efforts.

"With your approval, I will be escorting Abigail home," Hiram announced. No one dared to comment, but several nodded in agreement. He scanned their suspicious, tight-lipped, faces.

"Very well, then we will be going," he added. The Master of McDonnally Manor helped Abigail with her wrap and they left without further delay. As the door closed behind them, a telltale cheer resounded from the drawing room. The exiting couple smiled, making no acknowledgement of the disturbing outbreak to the other.

Once outside, Hiram offered Abigail his arm and they strolled across the cobblestones towards his estate. Now, still battling, this time side-by-side to maintain the bond, they went to great lengths in choosing their words, so as not to offend the other. Semantics and tone had played a large part in their previous ongoing war. Now, engaging words as weapons was, decidedly, a crime of the past. Hiram took the initiative to begin the conversation, handling the situation with kid gloves.

"Is the night air too chilling for you?" he asked.

"No, not at all, I find it to be quite refreshing," Abigail insisted.

"I do, as well."

"It was a pleasant visit," she remarked.

"Indeed, I can honestly say that I have never had a more gratifying experience."

"Me, either," Abigail added timidly.

"However, the Burns' Night celebration was uncommonly spectacular," Hiram mentioned casually.

"How so?"

"That is the night that my niece came into our lives."

"Was Sophia born on Burns' Night?"

"No, no," Hiram chuckled. "This past year, during the festivities, she arrived in Lochmoor for the first time, quite unexpectedly. Her mother is my twin sister."

Abigail stopped cold.

"Abigail, have I said something to offend you?"

"Hiram McDonnally, your sister is your *twin* and you never told me?" she stated with disappointment and disapproval. *Sophia never mentioned it either,* she thought, feeling slighted by her dear friend.

Hiram looked down at her, distracted by her appealing femininity, brilliantly enhanced in the moonlight.

"Now see here, Abby...we have not been on the best of terms of late...with exception to the last hour." His words softened, "Family relations was the last topic that one would have thought to discuss."

Abigail released his arm, mulling over his rationalization. She looked to his gentle dark eyes, put her anger in check, and took his arm. "That is quite all right, love."

Hiram smiled down with relief. They moved on.

"Do you care to discuss family relations, tonight, Hiram?"

"Not particularly, Abigail."

Abigail stopped abruptly.

"'Tis not that I do not wish to share that information with you, Abigail... shan't we confine our conversation to more pertinent subjects to our relationship... so that we might savor our last few minutes together?"

"Our last few minutes?" she said with apparent shock.

"Tonight, Abby, our last few minutes together, *tonight*."

"Oh, of course, Hiram."

Hiram patted her hand, rolled his eyes to the night sky. They continued down the road.

"Hiram?"

"Aye?"

"Why did you shave off your beard?"

"Why did you choose tonight to wear that French perfume for the first time?"

Abigail shrugged and dropped her head to the side to hide her embarrassment.

"Do you like my new face, Miss O'Leardon?"

"One would suspect, as much as you enjoy the fragrance."

They exchanged approving grins and moved together toward the estate. With their silence, the haunting wails of the red-throated divers in the loch echoed in the distance. The couple approached the portal of the mansion and Hiram opened the door. "Might you come in and take tea with me?" he teased.

"Sir, I would be delighted."

They entered the hall and Hiram helped Abigail remove her coat and placed it on the wall hook. Facing the archway, they were met with the surprise of a visitor occupying the divan in the parlor.

Hiram reacted spontaneously, "Do my eyes deceive me?" The sleeping beauty awoke and sat up.

"Sam, you are absolutely adorable!"

Abigail scrutinized the features of the dark-eyed, dark-haired woman whom she determined to be close to the same age as her escort. She naturally deduced the woman to be Hiram's twin and gave a sigh.

"Delilah, is it really you?" Hiram' asked, thrilled with her presence.

Delilah...Sam, Sampson. How quaint. Abigail smiled, pleased to be witnessing the timely family reunion.

"Yes, love, who else!" the woman beamed.

Hiram left Abigail, to embrace the guest. "How long has it been?"

"Only a year, Sam."

"It feels like a lifetime."

"Still the most handsome man to walk the earth, even *without* the distinguishing beard."

Interesting comment for a twin to make, but sweet, Abigail thought.

"Lilah, please," Hiram said sheepishly. Abigail smiled in agreement.

"Introduce me to your young friend, Sam," Delilah insisted.

"I beg your pardon, this is Abigail O'Leardon, my best friend's— other than you Lilah...my dear friend Daniel's sister. Abigail, may I present, Delilah, my dearest friend from Switzerland. Her father was my employer. Remember, I told you, I was an apprentice in clock repair? Her father was my mentor," he said proudly.

Abigail's smile quickly faded, overcome with shock and confusion. *Friend? Clock repair? Switzerland?* Having difficulty in concealing her instant feelings of betrayal and jealousy, Abigail began coughing violently.

Hiram rushed to aid her. "Abigail, are you all right?"

"Yes," she coughed once more. "Please excuse me, I will get some water from the kitchen," she said in a raspy voice.

"I can get it for you," Hiram offered. Abigail shook her head and fled down the hall.

"I hope she soon recovers," Delilah commented.

The sound of approaching hooves and clacking of the carriage wheels on the cobblestone drive brought an end to the visit.

"Sorry, Sam, I have to be going. Come with me, I want you to meet someone." She took Hiram's hand and led him out to the drive where a tall, thin, blonde-haired gentleman stepped out of the carriage.

"Sam, this is Starrett Highmore, my fiancé," Delilah introduced proudly. The two men shook hands.

"My pleasure, sir. Hiram McDonnally. Would you be related to the painter?" Hiram asked.

"Joseph Highmore? Nay, cannot say that I am. It would be a jolly good feather in my cap, if I were; I am in the business of architecture."

"And what is your professional opinion of this wee cottage, Starr? Sam is the grand master of this ostentatious estate," Delilah teased. "He has done pretty well for an apprentice clock repairman. Do you not agree?"

"Indeed," Starrett nodded as he admired the estate, helped his future bride into the carriage and then climbed in beside her. Hiram moved to the carriage door.

"Grand for you to visit, Delilah. Sorry, you could not have stayed a bit longer, I should have liked to become better acquainted with you, Mr. Highmore. I do congratulate you, sir, and assure you that you are guaranteed a life of contentment. You could not have chosen a more delightful wife," Hiram added.

"Thank you, Mr. McDonnally. I am well aware of my good fortune," Starrett squeezed his intended's hand.

"Now, Sam, do come for the wedding. Remember, December twentieth, at the little church in our village. You may bring a guest!"

"I am honored, thank you."

Back in the kitchen, Abigail stopped pouting, took a glass from the cupboard and filled it with water from the pitcher. With second thoughts of leaving Hiram alone with the temptress, she abandoned the unnecessary refreshment and returned to the parlor to face the threatening element of her new beau's past. In finding that they had vacated the parlor, she went directly to the hall where the sound of voices enticed her to the sidelight. In seeing Hiram, standing at the door of the carriage, Abigail cracked the door and listened.

"I miss you, Sam, and love you," Delilah said sweetly. Abigail's eyes narrowed with rage.

"I too, Lilah," Hiram returned.

Abigail, fuming with fury, closed the door with tightened fists and stomped her foot. She bypassed the kitchen and marched straight through to the back door and out into the moonlit garden. Her brewing anger was driving her pace to the back gate leading to the caretakers' cottage. Nearly out of control, she grasped the rails, clenching her teeth.

At the front of the estate, Delilah called out as the carriage pulled away, "You had better check on your guest and give her my regards!"

"I shall! Have a safe journey!" The passengers waved as Hiram watched a bit of his past diminish in the distance.

Meanwhile, the reunited young couple, Guillaume Zigmann and Allison O'Connor, were laughing and teasing the Wheaton children on the porch of the cottage, behind the mansion. Their merriment drove Abigail to the far side of the garden, facing the woods to Brachney Hall. Breathing hard and biting her bottom lip, she fought the tears, as she pressed her hands against the stonewall. She stared angrily at the black silhouetted branches, seemingly pointing at her with mockery for her naivety in believing that she could ever find a man whom she could trust.

"I am such a fool. I should have never trusted you! It was over before it began. I knew that it was too good to be true. I knew it!" She repeatedly slapped her hands down to the wall, proclaiming, "I should have never loved you,

Hiram McDonnally!"

Her hands stung with bruising pain. She stopped and brought her hands to her face and began to cry. *Dear God, why me?*

A stern voice behind her asked, "Truce?"

Abigail's sobs subsided when she peeked through her fingers to see a large white handkerchief dangling before her face. She slowly turned to find its owner standing before her. He gently wiped her cheeks with the flag of surrender and offered it to her. Her breathing became rapid. She ripped it from his hand.

"Truce! Have you lost your mind? You are a greater fool than I am, Master McDonnally! You imposter!"

"Abigail O'Leardon, you are the most confounded vexation! You continually try my patience! Do not let another word leave your mouth, until I have had my say!" Hiram roared, throwing his arms up with outrage.

Guillaume and Allison wasted no time in ushering the Wheaton children into the cottage.

Abigail stepped back. Hiram stared down at her, with his eyes blazing. Gradually regaining control of his incensed temper, he reached toward her and pulled the handkerchief from her hand. He gently wiped the tears from her cheeks.

"Now... enough tears. I cannot have my woman running off every few minutes in a jealous rage. For your information, Delilah came to Lochmoor to introduce me to her fiancé." Hiram's dark eyes demanded that she listen without objection. "The fact is, Miss O'Leardon, that you and I are bound to meet with those who stir the green-eyed monster. However, need I remind you that we have made a pact to trust one another?

Our treaty shan't be broken if we are to continue this relationship." Hiram spoke with conviction, albeit without compassion, as he found her display to be truly disappointing.

Abigail looked away to the pasture to escape his reprimanding presence.

"I will not coddle you, nor sympathize with your feminine tendencies on this subject. I find your behavior demeaning and consider it to be an exhibition of blatant mistrust in the feelings that I have professed for you."

Abigail stood motionless before him.

"Now, if you care to take tea with me, I will be in the parlor. If not, I bid you, good night."

Abigail was on the verge of retaliating when Hiram unexpectedly reached into his pocket and pulled out a single flower, which he had pilfered from the vase on the kitchen table. With a forgiving smile, enhanced by his endearing dimples, he touched it to her nose and handed it to her. He nodded, turned, and walked seemingly confident through the garden; however, he blew out a sigh of relief that Abigail had not flown off the handle with his scornful reproach.

She watched him leave, *Strange man. Naomi was right, his temper is not to be trifled with, even in matters of love.*

The master of the house walked back with a tinge of regret for his severe tone with Abigail, despite his knowing that he had to take a firm stand at this early stage of their relationship. Abigail stood motionless, refereeing the conflict between her injured pride and her over-powering urge to follow him. She reviewed his demands. Although she abhorred and resented his condescending attitude, she admired his determination to preserve their love. The question of his past relationship with Delilah remained to haunt her.

Abigail decided to relent and moved quickly through the garden maze. She opened the door to the back entrance of the mansion and stepped in on the small braided rug. Wiping her shoes and massaging her arms, chilled with the spring air, she peered down the hall. The mansion was quiet, with exception to the tick of the grandfather clock. The kitchen was dark, for it was late, nearly ten o'clock. The glowing light, flickering at the end of the hall, lured her to the parlor. Her footsteps shortened as she approached the archway.

He said that he loved me. *Did he really love* her, *before? Does he still have feelings for her? But, he did refer to me as "his woman". I have to know.*

Only a half dozen steps would deliver her to the point of no return. Abigail squinted in the dimly lit, hall mirror, repinned the sides of her hair and pulled on a curl dangling along side of her face. She took a breath of courage and entered the room. Hiram was squatting on the hearth before the dwindling fire, rearranging the logs with a poker.

"Come, warm yourself by the fire," he offered without standing to greet her. Abigail walked timidly toward him. Hiram stood and pulled a chair close to his. She sat down and he resumed his place across from her.

"How is your cough, Abigail?"

"Cough? Oh, yes. It seems to have dissipated."

"And your hands?" He leaned forward.

"My hands?" Abigail hesitated, unnerved by his eyes, twinkling in the firelight.

Hiram reached down, lifted her hands, and turned them to expose her palms. He examined them. They were still red from the scornful attack on the wall.

"Anger can be very destructive, my dear. I know, I am— *was* the expert on retaliation." He kissed her palms, not taking his eyes from hers. He filled the two teacups on the table beside him and handed her one, gently balanced on the saucer. She took it unable to escape his commanding gaze.

She took a sip, gathered her courage and then focusing on the teacup, she asked, "Hiram?"

"Yes, do you have a question, Abigail?"

"How well did you know her?" she looked directly at him.

"Is it really of consequence? I should not need to address this issue."

Abigail looked away, perturbed.

Hiram noted her displeasure. "Abigail, Delilah was a dear friend, when I had no one else in the world. She was very special and remains to be so."

How special? Abigail contemplated and then inquired, "A bit like a sister?"

"In all honesty, I cannot answer that question. I have never experienced the pleasure of having a sister."

Abigail's motivation to continue the questioning was momentarily lost in the pity she felt for Hiram and his estranged twin. She sat down her cup and walked over to the window. She stood in the shadows, silent and tense, reviewing her dilemma.

If I pursue this further, learning of his love for her, will mortify me. If I refrain, the unknown will haunt me the rest of my life. However, if their relationship was purely platonic, the relief will *restore my sanity.* Perspiration appeared on her sore palms with the dread of further inquiry to the relationship. She turned to see Hiram staring into the flames, and offering no assistance to her predicament. She knew that the relationship demanded no other recourse and that she could not postpone the inevitable. Hiram leaned back and stretched his legs, ignoring her. He ran his hand across his face unconsciously seeking the absent familiar beard.

"Abigail," he addressed her with his focus on the fire, "your tea is becoming cold."

She left the safety of the distant corner to move into the ring, aware of his volatile temper and intolerance for jealousy. She passed behind his chair, walked directly in front of him, and stared down at him. Hiram was about to comment on her return, when she spoke, praying that she had made the right decision.

"Curiosity and inquiry to the past need not be misconstrued as jealousy," she defended.

"Aye," Hiram listened with suspicion.

"However, if one does experience *jealousy,* perhaps it is the result of failure of one's partner to make one feel secure in the relationship," Abigail cautiously suggested.

Hiram leaned toward her, ready to explode when Abigail quickly added, "Jealousy might be considered a blessing of sorts."

Hiram's brows knitted with confused anger, "A blessing, Abigail?"

"Jealousy is proof positive that one has genuine feelings... for someone," Abigail reasoned.

Hiram left the chair, "Abigail, are you telling me that you needed a tinge of jealousy to prove that you and I shared something special?" he said with annoyance.

This comment did not set well with her.

"No, no, no! You are distorting my words!" she blurted in frustration. "Stop toying with me, Hiram McDonnally! I do not care if you ever tell me! Have your petty secrets! I understand perfectly!" She turned abruptly and headed for the door. Hiram followed and caught her arm.

"Abigail, stop. Stop, right now." He turned her around. His touch took her off guard and she held her chin tight to her chest. He guided her to the divan and pulled her down beside him.

"Please look at me and listen to every word." Abigail looked up, exhausted by the tension and distress, which she had created.

"What do you desire for me to say, that I never loved another woman? I can tell you any lie which you may care to hear, but you are well aware that I was once in love with Naomi," he said sternly. Abigail's eyes welled up.

In seeing her response, Hiram lowered his voice to a comforting tone. "Abby, everyone wants to be the first love and the last, but it seldom happens that way." He took her hand in his. "Abby, you may not be the first woman in my life, but you are the only one, now, and that sets you far above the rest. What happened yesterday or years ago is insignificant. You are the woman in my dreams, the woman that has taught me that *love* is worth every struggling minute of a relationship. Abby, your fears are *truly* unfounded. I think that you know, that if I did not choose to be with you, we would not be sitting here, tonight."

Abigail's downcast expression remained unchanged. She stared blankly at her hand in his and said nothing. Her indifference to his explanation, led Hiram to leave the divan with frustration. He walked a few steps away, and then turned to her and blurted out.

"Do you want the truth? Very well!" He began pacing and speaking as though he were standing before the High Court. "We met shortly after I arrived in Switzerland, when I was seventeen. Only *seventeen*, Abigail. We became good friends while I worked as an apprentice to her father. Delilah found that I was becoming attracted to her...but only out of my loss of Naomi...I tried desperately to fill that void. Delilah knew that it was not my attraction to her that sought her attention, but rather the idea of having someone with whom to share my life."

Hiram pulled the rocker close to the divan and sat before Abigail to insure her attentiveness. He continued, "She was graciously understanding at the time and explained that she did not share the same feelings for me. From that day forward, we were best of friends."

Hiram leaned back for a moment then returned, close to Abigail. "I admit that at first, my ego was in ill repair, but in time, I concentrated on my work and set the entire incident behind me." Hiram fell back with satisfaction for his thorough explanation. "There, are you feeling better?" Abigail sat silently staring at the floor.

Hiram slapped his knees and stood up. "My confession was obviously not sufficient. Perhaps, if I told you that I intend to take a short leave of absence, you would be convinced."

Abigail reacted with alarm, "You are leaving, to be with *her*?"

"*Abigail,* have you not heard a word that I have said? Yes, I am leaving. I have business to which I need to attend." He walked a few steps away and then faced her. "When I return, there is a certain brother of a certain young lady with whom I need to speak of a rather serious matter."

"You are going to speak with Daniel?" she said suspiciously.

Hiram's scowl transcended into a clever smile. "Is that not the traditional procedure? I *am* a stranger to these arrangements."

"Hiram!" Abigail, freed from all her jealous fears, flew from her seat and threw her arms around his neck. She placed a kiss on his cheek, and then bounded through the parlor through the archway and up the stairs. *Thank you, God! Thankyouthankyouthankyou!* "Sophia! Sophia!"

Hiram returned to his original place by the fire, and placed his feet upon the chair across from him.

"I congratulate you, Mr. McDonnally, and assure you, that you are guaranteed a life of... *contentment*? You could not have chosen a more... "extraordinary" wife."

Hiram closed his eyes, smiled and shook his head.

"Ah love, let us be true
To one another!
for the world, which seems
To lie before us like a land of dreams."

—Matthew Arnold

Chapter 11

"Mother"

"From mirror after mirror,
No vanity's displayed:
I'm looking for the face I had
Before the world was made."

—William Butler Yeats

Monday morning, Hiram left his estate shortly before dawn, while Daniel arranged to take Naomi back to London for purchases for her upcoming wedding. Edward was left in the care of the gardener, Angus, while Abigail was to remain at McDonnally Manor on an extended holiday with Sophia.

Albert drove Hiram to the village where he engaged a carriage to deliver him to the Manchester train station. Watching the morning awake on the moors, Hiram sat content with thoughts of requesting Abigail's hand in marriage. Although she was well into her twenties, Hiram insisted on following proper protocol in asking Daniel's permission. He slid his fingers over his clean-shaven chin. *Abigail McDonnally, aye, she will be a good wife, a trifle feisty, but never a bore.* He leaned back, peering out the carriage window. *A bit headstrong— life with her may be a challenge. I hope I can... no, I will maintain control.* "I anticipate no difficulty because I love her and she loves me; that is the important factor, like Edward and Naomi." He smiled and looked out the window. His smile faded, "Perhaps, not quite."

Later that week, the forlorn face of a woman appeared at a veiled window overlooking London's Baker Street. Beyond the sun-scorched curtains, a couple of older girls giggled in the street below. The woman's eyes, dull with despair, watched as the young women rushed past three male peers who were offering unsolicited comments to the strollers' feminine beauty.

"Bea, whatcha starin' at?" a gruff voice demanded. "Get away from that window!"

Examining the girls' stylish dress and their youthful smiles, her heart ached with regret, knowing that she had missed the blossoming years of her only daughter, Naomi.

Her reddening face turned slowly with contempt and responded, "Have you not taken enough from me? Now, you deny me the chance to view a thread of life of the free?" she asked wearily.

"Blast ye, ye ungrateful wench! I hae given ye all the necessities o' life and more. Look in the glass, hag. What hae ye given me? Look at yerself—nay, ye are a bloomin' disaster, not 'alf as tolerable as when we met," he snarled.

"Met?" she retorted. "Has it been so many years that you are denying that you kidnapped me?"

"Ye wanted to be wit' me. No one regrets it more than meself!"

Incensed, she rose to her feet and pointed her finger at her captor with defiance, "I fought you tooth and nail! No, you needed me, to save your cowardly skin!"

"Shut yer mouth woman! I wouldna be interested in yer twisted view. Do ye take me for a fool? Ye'd gone directly to Scotland Yard!" he sneered.

"I had promised my silence, if you would have freed me," she replied, exhausted from the confrontation.

"If ye wanted to leave, why did ye stay, ye ungrateful leach?" He glowered.

The door to the flat opened, "Hello, Mother, I brought fruit from the market."

"Thank you, Henry," Beatrice kissed the forehead of the tall, young man. Still reeling from the confrontation, she displayed a half-hearted smile and placed the fruit in the basket on the table.

"Mother, are you ill?"

"No son."

"Pearl and your grandsons send their love. They drew these pictures for you." He handed Beatrice the precious drawings. The unidentifiable scribbling brought a tear to her eye.

"They are beautiful, son."

"They cannot wait to see you, Mother."

"I know son, I miss them too. Thank them for the lovely artwork, dear."

"Shall you return for another visit before autumn, Mother?"

"Henry, I fear that we shall be in London for only a few more days, this year."

Her son looked disapprovingly at his father and pulled an envelope from his vest pocket. "This is from Dirth."

The hefty man snatched the letter and wandered to the other side of the room to read it.

"Henry, you are missing a button," Beatrice noticed.

"No, I am not, it is here in my pocket, Mother."

"Please, fetch my sewing box from the pantry shelf." Henry lifted down the quilted round box, a Christmas gift from the grandsons.

"Take off your coat and give it to me, son," Beatrice insisted.

"Ye coddle him like a bairn— he has a wife. If yer mendin', mend me trousers," his father grumbled as he folded the letter and placed it in his pocket.

"I will mend anything that I see fit. Which pocket is the button in, Henry?"

"The inside pocket, Mother."

"Ah, yes, I am glad that you kept it. This is an

unusual one, difficult to replace." She turned the button over in her palm then opened the padded lid of the case. Nearly a dozen threaded needles neatly lined the top of the box.

"Always prepared, Mother?" Henry sat next to his mother observing the spread of needles. "Remember the time that I mended the sofa?" Henry teased.

"I certainly do. You were no more than a lad of four or five. You used every single one of my needles and stitched here and there and everywhere."

"Aye, blast ye, Henry! I took one in here," his father pointed at his posterior. Henry turned away and smiled with satisfaction.

"Serves you right for returning drunk," Beatrice remarked sharply.

"Ye be watchin' yer tongue, woman, I work me fingers to the bone for ye. I will reward meself with a bit of ale, whenever I get the notion!"

Beatrice responded with disgust, "Cecil, you have never worked a month straight in your life."

"Why ye—" with agitation he moved toward his battered wife, who acted with little regard to his threats and continued with her mending.

Henry instinctively intervened. "If you so much as lay a hand on her," the young man warned with a foreboding glare. His father backed away.

Beatrice knotted the thread and trimmed the fine threads with the tiny scissors. "There you go, son." She quickly handed the garment to him.

"Thank you, Mother. Pearl will appreciate it, as much as I do; she is very busy these days."

Cecil growled and moved to the window. "Busy? Doin' what?"

Beatrice grabbed her son's wrist, "No son,

ignore him."

Henry's father pulled his pipe from his coat pocket and tapped it on his hand. "They're waitin' for me at the pub, ye stay put, I shan't be back tonight," he snarled and left the flat.

After Cecil left, Henry kissed his mother's forehead and left to continue with his errands. Beatrice slid the tattered curtain aside, watching for her son. A minute later, the young man was waving and smiling up at her. She forced a grin and gestured her farewell. Her grim expression followed his turning the corner, out of sight. Henry was the light of her life and her inspiration to face her dreary world of uneventful days. Beatrice clung to her faith and the belief that Henry was a God-given gift, although his conception was without her consent.

You will understand. I love you, Henry. I will see you later.

A middle-aged couple, walking hand-in-hand replaced his form in the street below. Beatrice envied their obvious loving relationship and their freedom to venture through town. She dropped the hem of the curtain, went directly to the bureau and stood before the antique etched mirror. She cocked her head, examining her likeness. *A little powder and a touch of lip rouge. The hair? Perhaps...*

"Hmm, a change of style, that is what I need."

She opened the top drawer and pulled out a small black coin purse from beneath a stack of neatly folded handkerchiefs. She took several hairpins from the little pocketbook and began twisting and lifting the wisps of silver and auburn strands into a variety of arrangements. Beatrice worked diligently. In a short while, she smiled satisfactorily, admiring her creation. The contented reflection caught her attention with noted surprise, for moments of joy were seldom and restricted to those cherished events with her son and his family.

The new coiffure demanded a change in attire. After rummaging through the trunk of worn, apparel, Beatrice dropped back on her heels with disgust. Her glare left the rubble, shifting to the cupboard across the room. She approached it slowly as though it possessed the power to draw her in, against her will. She knelt down, opened the lower door, and reached to the back of the lower shelf. She removed a brown package, tied with string, closed the cupboard door and carried the treasure to the table. She began untying the parcel with reverence.

Her fingers caressed the delicate lace trim and sash of the navy blue dress. She admired the fine fabric, remembering the morning of Henry's wedding day when he lovingly presented it to her. Not only had she experienced the rare opportunity to don the beautiful gift and stand proudly with her son, but she did it alone, untainted with *his* presence; Cecil, spent the wedding day frequenting the local pubs, avoiding Pearl's side of the family. Matters of matrimony were alien to him, being an orphan and having no desire to marry the mother of his child.

Beatrice lifted the dress and held it up, reminiscing with delight. She stared at the dress for a minute, struggling with the decision, and then gave into her impulse. She dropped the dress to the table, looked at her pendant watch with contempt. *Time may be running out. What if he returns?* She unpinned the watch, unbuttoned the faded gray dress and dropped it to the floor. She slipped on the dress, buttoned it quickly, and attached the watch. The dull black shoes sneered up at her.

"You were handsome, four years ago. I wish that I could have kept you with the dress, but that probably would have meant going barefoot."

She went over to the basin, dampened a cloth, and ran it over the tops of the scuffed shoes. They had served her well, but time had taken its toll on *them*, as well. Her expression was resolute and impenetrable.

"No matter, I will not spend another day locked up, like the criminal that he is. His behavior merits confinement, not mine!"

She pulled the carpetbag from beneath the bed, chose a few outfits from the trunk, folded them and placed them in the bag with other necessities. She tossed the remaining clothes back into the trunk and slammed it closed. After adding her holy book, an envelope of stamps, the collection of Henry's letters, and half dozen handkerchiefs to her bag, she snatched the black coin purse and the tiny bottle of toilet water and stuffed them into her pocketbook. Beatrice moved directly to the pantry and retrieved her sewing box, a cloth-covered box of photographs, the cherished drawings, and the fruit.

Her movements transcended from erratic and desperate, to cautious and deliberate, as she approached the small tin box sitting behind the cracker jar on the wall shelf. *He warned me, opening that tin without his permission would result in severe repercussions.* She opened the jar, knowing that there was no turning back, removed half of its contents, and replaced the lid. She took the wad of bills and hastily tucked them into her pocketbook. She pulled on her coat and with the landlady's mending in one arm and her bag on the other, she made one quick scan and closed the door to a life of brutal incarceration.

My life is mine.

Beatrice rushed down to the flat below and rapped urgently. An elderly woman responded.

"Beatrice, come in."

"Only for a minute, Mrs. Pendleton, I need your assistance. Here is your mending."

"Thank you. I see that you finally got your nerve," she smiled pointing at the bag.

"Yes, not a moment to soon, either."

"I am proud of you. How much time do you have, before he returns?"

"I am not certain, the sooner I disappear, the better. May I please have a piece of paper to write a short note to my son and could you please post it for me today? I do not want Henry returning and confronting Cecil."

"Yes, come in the dining room, I will fetch your pay, as well. You are doing the right thing, Beatrice. This is best for you and Henry. He will no longer have reason to see his father. His contempt for Cecil is quite apparent." Mrs. Pendleton handed Beatrice the payment for the mending and directed to her a small desk. Beatrice placed the cash into her pocketbook, sat down and chose a piece of paper from the basket of stationery.

"Henry is a good man," Beatrice said proudly as she dipped the pen and scribbled the note. She placed it in an envelope and addressed it.

"I will seal it for you."

"Here. Thank you Mrs. Pendleton, I will miss you and shall be forever indebted to you. You gave me my sanity with your comforting talks these few weeks past."

"Keep in touch, Beatrice."

"I shall. I must go now. Thank you for everything." The two women exchanged teary-eyed hugs before Beatrice rushed out of the flat to the street.

"Take care!" Mrs. Pendleton called.

"I shall!"

Chapter 111

"The Escape"

"With fingers weary and worn,
With eyelids heavy and red
A woman sat in unwomanly rags
Plying her needle and thread."

—Thomas Hood

On London's west side, Naomi, entered the neatly organized haberdasher in search of lace and ribbon to decorate Brachney Hall for her wedding reception. Naomi went to the area displaying the fabric and sewing notions where she noticed a young man in his twenties, examining a bolt of fabric of blue and gray plaid. Naomi found that the young shopper was experiencing some difficulty in choosing between the fabric he held and one with a striped pattern. Naomi continued comparing the various spools of ribbon, until her motherly instinct to assist led her to speak with the gentleman.

"Excuse me, sir; is there something that I might help you with? I am an experienced seamstress." The man smiled with some embarrassment.

"Possibly, I need some fabric to make shirts for my young sons." Naomi's heart opened to the stranger, imagining the young father to be a widower and left to sew for his children.

"Have you sewn many articles of clothing for them?" she asked curiously with sympathy.

"I have endeavored to sew only once," he chuckled.

"I beg your pardon, but making a shirt is quite an undertaking, if you have not sewn one," Naomi gently explained.

"I am sure that it is. To be more specific, my only experience with mending was one in which I mischievously invaded my mother's sewing box and stitched up the sofa."

"Oh, my, I am sure that your mother was a bit annoyed."

"Although I was but four years old at the time, I shall never forget the look on her face. I am not certain as to which angered her more, my upholstery repair or the fact that I had used all of her threaded needles." He picked up the striped bolt. "I am purchasing the fabric for my wife to make the shirts. I guess this one is appropriate for young boys. Do you agree?"

Naomi's cheery smile vanished and now, she stood frozen, staring into the eyes of the stranger. She shivered as a chill sped through her body. She became lightheaded and weak-kneed. *Can it be? Could it be?*

"Madame, are you ill?" the concerned man asked, reaching to aid her. Naomi steadied herself against the large shelf and swallowed hard.

"What did you say?" she mumbled.

"I asked if you were ill."

"No...the needles," Naomi, asked wearily.

The store manager appeared and helped Naomi to a chair in the next aisle. "Mrs. McDonnally, may I fetch you a glass of water? You appear faint."

At this point Naomi's head was spinning. She had foregone breakfast and the stress of the earlier conversation further nauseated her already empty stomach. The manager insisted that he would tend to Naomi's needs and that the young customer should proceed to the counter to have the fabric cut by the assistant.

"I hope you are soon feeling better, Madame," the stranger remarked as he headed to the front of the store caring the bolt of striped fabric.

Naomi closed her eyes, trying to restore her composure. She strained to listen to the muffled conversation between the young man and the assistant, which was barely audible above the crinkling of the brown paper used to wrap the fabric and the chattering of two older women who entered the store. Naomi tried to make sense of the man's comments and stood to locate him. She caught a glimpse of him passing through the aisles toward the door when she heard Vivian, the assistant, call out to him.

"Tell your mother, that I send my regards!"

"I shall," he returned.

Naomi immediately sought to ask the manager about the stranger, but he had moved to the stationery section where he was reprimanding the very same, dirty, little boy of whom Naomi had spoken to Edward about, only a week earlier. Naomi moved through the rows of linens to the window. Seeing no sign of the young man, she continued on to the front counter.

"Vivian, the young man that purchased the fabric, do you know him?" Naomi asked impatiently.

"Yes, he comes in occasionally to purchase fabric for his wife."

"What is his name?"

"I have no idea."

"Oh..." Naomi's heart sank with disappointment. She turned to walk away.

"Did you care to make a purchase, Mrs. McDonnally?"

"I nearly forgot...just some ribbons and lace." Naomi wandered back to the notions. She chose two spools of ribbon and one of white lace and returned to the counter.

"What lengths, Mrs. McDonnally?"

"I would like to purchase the entire spools, thank you." Naomi answered despondently.

"Preparing for your wedding?"

"Yes."

"So very romantic, I must say. If I had the opportunity to renew my vows, I am not certain that my husband would," Vivian said jokingly.

Noting Naomi's preoccupation, Vivian asked, "Mrs. McDonnally, if I might inquire, what is your interest in the young man?"

"It was a comment that he made in regard to his mother."

"What did he say?"

"He mentioned 'threaded needles'...did you make reference to his mother?" Naomi asked anxiously.

"Yes, I did."

"Then you know her? What is her name?" Naomi's voice rose with excitement.

"Please, calm down, Mrs. McDonnally, the customers."

"Please, Vivian, what is her name?"

"Mrs. McDonnally, I would like to help you, but I do not know her name."

"But, you said—"

"I met her one morning a year ago. We had a nice conversation. She was visiting for only a few days and came into the store with her son to purchase... thread and buttons, I believe. We never got around to formally introducing ourselves."

"Do you remember her appearance?"

Vivian stared curiously at Naomi and answered deep in thought, "Come to think of it, strangely, she looked a bit like you, Mrs. McDonnally."

Have my prayers been answered? Is my mother alive? Naomi's heart pounded erratically.

"Shall I ask the young man of his mother's name, if he returns? I cannot guarantee that it shall be anytime soon; he is not one of our regular customers. He only visits the store infrequently, a couple times a year."

"Please, Vivian."

"Certainly, Mrs. McDonnally. Where would you like me to send the information, to your new home in Lochmoor?"

"If you could, please address and send it to me at McDonnally Manor in Lochmoor Glen, I would greatly appreciate it."

"Even if it is not for six months?"

"Even if it is six years from now, Vivian," Naomi commanded. Vivian looked at Naomi curiously. Naomi made her purchase, thanked Vivian and left the store in a daze.

Threaded needles...my mother is the only woman that I have ever known to have threaded needles in her sewing box. But how many women are there in this world with sewing boxes? Moreover, how many thread their needles beforehand, but how many look like me?

She removed her hankie from her pocketbook and wiped her eyes. Naomi headed to the quaint London cottage for the last time, scanning every face that she passed.

Meanwhile, mixed feelings of euphoric freedom and dreaded fear of her soon to be irate captor, urged Beatrice on. She entered the street with caution and stealth and headed for the square with the intent to purchase train fare. After several minutes, she paused in front of the bookstore and sat her bag at her feet to give her weary arm a much-needed rest. The window display caught her eye. Beatrice moved closer to get a better view of a mystery novel with a large postage stamp embossed on the leather cover. Inside the shop, the proprietor spotted the potential customer admiring his display. He exited to promote the sale.

Daniel O'Leardon approached Beatrice and found her face to be strangely familiar.

"Madame, would ye care to be takin' a closer look at that fine volume?" He looked at her curiously, trying to place the face.

Beatrice reached down and grabbed the handle of her bag. "No thank you, sir. I need to be getting along." Beatrice looked down the street toward the flat when her eyes widened fearfully in seeing Cecil entering the building. *Why is he returning so soon? The pipe! He was out of tobacco, he has returned for money to buy the tobacco. The jar!*

Her fearful reaction led Daniel to inquire, "Will ya not come in for a bit, where ya can take a closer look?"

She turned hastily and replied, "Yes, yes, I would like to come in."

Daniel opened the door and ushered her into the store. Beatrice entered, looking over her shoulder, watching the door.

"Here, here is the volume." Daniel took a copy and handed it to the distracted customer. "Madame?"

The bell jingled over the door. Beatrice's heart stopped as she slipped quickly behind a bookcase. Oliver, Daniel's assistant anxiously entered the store, carrying a stack of boxes.

"Mr. O'Leardon, there is a daft man down the street! He is raising quite a ruckus, searching frantically for a thief!"

Daniel looked over at Beatrice peeking from behind the shelf.

"Oliver, we shall be closin' early today. I have

business to be attendin' to."

"Sir?"

"Oliver, give me the boxes, pull the shade, turn the sign and draw the curtain at the window!"

"Yes, sir."

"Ya may leave by way o' the backdoor. I shall be seein' ya tomorrow." Daniel placed the boxes on the counter. Oliver performed his duties without further inquiry or knowledge of Beatrice's presence.

"Good day, Mr. O'Leardon."

"Thank ya, Oliver and good day to ya."

Once Oliver had safely gone, Beatrice crept out from behind the shelving.

"Madame, would this man be lookin' for ya?"

Beatrice fearfully whispered, "Yes, sir."

"Is he yer husband?"

"No, sir."

"Have ya stolen from this man?"

"Absolutely not! I only took my fair share!"

"So yer in danger?"

"For years," Beatrice said stoically.

Daniel realized the circumstances of the relationship to which Beatrice was alluding. "Then we shall be needin' to get movin', news travels fast."

"I need to purchase fare."

"We shall see what we can do," Daniel said reassuringly, guiding her to the backroom.

They stopped at the dreaded rapping at the door.

Chapter IV

"Nightfall"

"I says, "me charming creature,
My joy, my heart's delight
How far have you to travel,
This dark and dreary night?"

"Do ya trust me?" Daniel whispered. Beatrice looked to Daniel's kind face and nodded. He took her hand and placed the key to his flat into it. "Go out the back and up the side stairs to me flat. I shall get rid o' him and join ya in a few minutes."

"Thank you, sir."

"Dun't be thankin' me yet. Now hurry on!"

The fervent rapping sent Beatrice flying to the backdoor while Daniel leisurely crossed the shop to the front door.

"Hold on!" Daniel called, and then lifted the shade. "Me shop is closed."

"I would be lookin' for a woman!"

"Are we not all? I am sorry to say there are no women in here, despite me many attempts."

"Open this bloomin' door!"

"Very, well." Daniel slowly unlatched the door. Cecil stormed in.

"Where is she? I know she is here!" He headed to the back room. Beatrice, now safely upstairs in Daniel's flat, listened through an air vent in the floor.

"And who might that be?" Daniel inquired.

"A thief! She has stolen me money!"

"And how would ya be describin' this thief?"

"A hag wit' a bag!" Cecil spouted.

"I have ne'er seen the likes o' such a woman. Ah, but I did see a quite beautiful woman earlier. She stopped in but for a minute." Beatrice smiled appreciatively, for the compliment.

"Yer lyin'! Where is she? I'll skin her alive when I find her!" Cecil shouted in Daniel's face.

Daniel reddened with fury. He grabbed Cecil by the collar and pulled him in closer. "Ya dun't want to be raisin' yer voice at me, man," he threatened. Cecil pulled from Daniel's grasp, blaspheming under his breath, ranting out of the shop. Daniel locked the door without delay and exited out the back to his flat to speak with the runaway. He knocked gently and beckoned, "Madame, 'tis me, Daniel, the shopkeeper."

Beatrice cautiously unbolted the door. Daniel entered, locking the door behind him. After the mayhem in the shop, Daniel's sunlit, silent flat offered an almost mystical atmosphere. The two strangers curiously stared at one another. The light accentuated Daniel's gentle face. He stepped forward, "Daniel, Daniel O'Leardon, at your service."

"Hello, I am..." Beatrice lowered her head.

Daniel cut in, "No need for names. How often do we use 'em in speakin', anyway?" He went over to the window overlooking the street. "Ah, he is makin' inquiries up and down the street. Would be best, if ya sit for a bit." He offered Beatrice a chair. She had prayed for assistance and it appeared the Almighty had delivered her to the protection of this freckle-faced, guardian angel.

"Sir...Daniel, I do not know what to say. Your kindness and generosity are far greater than I deserve."

"Yer quite welcome, but ya need not be thankin' me. I should be thankin' ya for cuttin' me workday short. Now, since the public establishments shan't be to our likin', I shall be preparin' a bite to eat." Daniel went to the cupboard of his tiny kitchen to gather ingredients to begin the meal.

"I owe you an explanation, Daniel."

"Tis not necessary. Just bein' a good neighbor." Daniel continued with the preparations.

"He is not my husband."

"I believed ya, the first time ya told me."

"I...I had his child. My boy is a good man, not at all like his father."

"He must take after his mother. Where is the lad?"

"He lives outside of town. He and his wife, Pearl, have two wonderful children, my grandsons," Beatrice said proudly. "I would have left years ago, but I had no money, no rela...no relations. I was not about to abandon my son, not again."

Daniel looked at her curiously. "Again?"

"Not Henry... are you married, Daniel?" Beatrice defensively changed the subject.

"Nay," he stirred the soup now bubbling on the stove, "I let the opportunity slip through me fingers into the hands o' another man."

"I am sorry."

"Me own fault, but I have had Abby to keep me company."

"Abby?"

"Me younger sister. Not for long, though. Me best friend has taken a fancy to her and she wi' him." Daniel ladled out two bowls of soup. "I am happy for 'em." He looked at the two bowls. He handed one to Beatrice, with a piece of day old bread.

"I raised Abby after me father and Abby's mother, me stepmother, were killed in the train collision at Armagh. It happened a few days before Abby's second birthday. Disastrous, eighty poor souls met the Almighty that day. Aye, it has been only the two o' us for years." He handed Beatrice a spoon.

"That is very honorable, Daniel."

"I am not certain o' that. I had sent her to the south o' England for schoolin'. Ah, for many a year, we corresponded, but I only had money enough to visit her but once every few months."

"She must love you very much."

"Abby is a very special lassie, I am the fortunate one." Daniel took a sip of his soup. "Life alone is tolerable enough. I have learned to live quite efficiently... vicariously, through me books and the fortune o' others."

"That is not *living*, Daniel. It is a fabricated existence. I know, I share in your expertise."

"What prevents ya from joinin' your son, Henry and his family?"

"Oh, I would never impose upon them. Besides, his father would, never permit it. He expects me to be his servant."

Daniel made no further comment on the subject. They continued their meal on a lighter note, to the mastery of Daniel's delightful anecdotes depicting young Oliver's apprenticeship. The couple laughed together over the last few bites and shared in clearing away the dishes. Beatrice sat temporarily content under the umbrella of security that Daniel offered, never once doubting his genuine sincerity.

Daniel placed the last bowl in the cupboard when Beatrice announced, "I thank you for your assistance and delightful meal, but now, I must be on my way." She crossed the room to gather up her coat and bag.

"Ya believe that I would allow ya to return to the streets with that madman, out there? We need to be makin' a plan," Daniel said with authority.

"We? I truly believe that you have done all that you can do for me, Daniel."

"He'll be watchin' the ticket office. I have a carriage. I know I am but a stranger, but I am offerin' ya a safe journey, to a bit o' sanctuary. Me cousin Rupert and his family have a cottage in Manchester. They are good, God fearin' people. They could put ye up for a few days. Rupert could drive ya into Manchester, when yer ready."

"Mr. O'Leardon, I would not think of further imposing on you and your kin," Beatrice shook her head.

"Ya shan't be imposin', ya would be doin' me cousin's wife, Laura, a favor. She doesna see another woman, but once every fortnight when Rupert takes her into town." Daniel took another peek out the window. "Madame, we had better leave by nightfall if we're to get there before midnight. We shan't disturb Rupert, he'll be readin' into the wee hours of the mornin'. The sooner we leave London, the better. Do ya care to catch a few winks before we leave? Yer welcome to take me sister's room." Beatrice looked toward the vacant room. "There is a bolt on the door," Daniel reassured, "and ya shan't be offendin' me by usin' it."

You are quite an agreeable man, Daniel O'Leardon, and yes, I feel perfectly safe with you.

"C'mon, ya need not be standin' there like a Machrie Moore Stone. Ya need yer rest." Daniel opened the door presenting the modest bedroom. "I'll be knockin' in a couple hours."

"Thank you, Daniel."

Beatrice sat her bag and pocketbook on the chair next to the bed. The room was quite small, but offered a pleasant welcoming atmosphere. She sat down on the edge of the bed, removed the tired black shoes, and lay down on the featherbed mattress. The late afternoon light peeked through the seam of the scarlet curtains. The fleur de lis pattern on the wallpaper stirred Beatrice's imagination with the unusual patterns presenting a variety of faces, appearing to question her presence. At the foot of the bed, another pair of framed faces, caught her eye. The sepia photograph was that of a serious, younger Daniel standing behind the seated figure of a mischievous-looking, young girl. Beatrice left the bed to get a closer look. *He has such a friendly face. The girl must be Abigail.* Beatrice returned to the bed and closed her eyes. Although the near miss with Cecil was fatiguing and the indefinite future taunted her, Beatrice was resting peacefully within a few minutes.

Daniel sat at the little table by the kitchen window and tapped his fingers lightly, planning the trip to his cousin's home. *I shall fetch me horse and carriage from the livery after wakenin' her. We shall ride to Oxford, and then take the train to Manchester. Such a lovely woman. She reminds me of someone...Naomi, aye, Naomi. How dare he be treatin' her wi' malice!*

He went to the sideboard and took inventory of the foodstuffs available for the journey. The next quarter hour he spent composing a short note to Oliver, explaining his absence and the importance of discretion in the matter. Daniel placed the pencil on the table and leaned back.

Imagine, a wonderful woman in the next room. All those years that I spent pinin' o'er Ellie. He reached over and spun the pencil. *Ellie...I wonder if she found the ribbon. What was she thinkin' when she found it?* His content expression transformed into one of dead seriousness. *Albert...he is a good husband to Ellie; I need to be lettin' go.* He snapped the pencil in half.

Bam, bam, bam! A sudden pounding at the door nearly gave Daniel cause to jump out of his skin. His thoughts fled to the frustrated vermin seeking his precious stow away.

"Open up, Daniel O'Leardon! This is Captain Sherbrooke."

Daniel hesitated, fearful for his guest's safety. He knew that he had no recourse and reluctantly opened the door.

"Good evenin', sir."

"Good evening, Daniel. Sorry to be troubling you at this hour, but this man says that his wife went into your shop this afternoon and never reappeared."

"Ye kidnapped her, ye did! I have witnesses!"

The constable interrupted, "Here, here, I shall handle this. Daniel, might I come in and end this malarkey?"

"Certainly, if ya would please be keepin' yer voices down, me sister, Abigail, could be sleepin'. She's not feelin' like herself."

The captain stepped inside, looked around and turned to Cecil, "You are mistaking, man. Give my regards to Abigail," he respectfully lowered his voice, "hope we did not wake her." The constable led Cecil away, unconvinced of Daniel's innocence in the matter. Daniel closed the door with a sigh of relief and turned to find Beatrice standing in the doorway of the bedroom.

"This has gone too far, Daniel. Now, I have involved you with the law, lying on my behalf, no less. I am leaving." Beatrice gathered her belongings.

"Yer not alone in this; I said I would help ya and that I shall do. I am a man o' me word. I shall hear no more 'bout it. I am goin' to fetch me carriage and leave this note for Oliver. I shan't be gone long. Please pack the basket wit' the food on the table and fetch the blankets from the bedroom shelf. Keep the door locked till I return." Daniel closed the door and was satisfied to hear the bolt slide into position.

He returned to the flat, pleased to find Beatrice packed and ready to go. Behind the shop, Daniel loaded the carriage and without conversation, the two set out for Oxford through the backstreets of London.

Once they were moving swiftly down the country roads, Daniel spoke.

"Pleasant evenin' for a ride... for a positive beginnin'."

"Yes, it is very pleasant."

They exchanged modest smiles, neither of whom imagined more appealing company with whom to share the journey.

"When sorrow wring thy gentle heart
O wilt thou let me cheer thee?
By the treasure of my soul,
That's the love I bear thee!"

—Robert Burns

Chapter V

"The Cottage"

"A guardian angel
o'er his life presiding,
Doubling his pleasures,
and his cares dividing."

—Samuel Rogers

After leaving, his horse and carriage at the Oxford livery, Daniel purchased the tickets to Manchester. Beatrice struggled to pay for hers, but Daniel stubbornly ignored her pleadings. On the train to Manchester, they became comfortably acquainted. Naturally, their conversation began with the usual small talk about the weather, followed by a running social commentary on current events, ranging from Joe Jeanette's boxing victories to Sara Bernhardt's Legion Of Honor Award. Finally, Daniel and Beatrice relaxed to discussion on a more personal level.

"It must be thrilling to order new titles and read them as they come in," Beatrice began.

"Me time to preview is limited. There is a lot o' work to be done in the shop."

"I imagine so. Have you owned the shop for a very long time?"

"Long enough, to want to be takin' a holiday from it."

"I cannot think of a more pleasant job. I adore books, Daniel."

"Aye?"

"Oh, yes, I have always been an avid reader. Do you dress your windows or do you hire a dresser and do you decorate for holidays and special events?" Beatrice asked with enthusiasm.

Daniel chuckled, "I am not much for decoratin'. I leave that to Oliver, which sometimes I come to regret."

"I see, have you ever..." Beatrice stopped.

"Aye? Tell me what's on yer mind," Daniel encouraged.

"I was wondering if you ever designed your windows with a particular theme: biographies, world explorers, or gardening, perhaps?"

"Odd that ya made mention o' that. Presently, I am preparin' a special event for Shakespeare's birthday," Daniel proudly announced.

"How creative."

"I have yet to put it all together. Thinkin' about servin' cake, and invitin' an actin' troupe to perform a few skits."

"Wonderfully clever, Daniel."

Daniel smiled at her approval.

In Manchester, Daniel rented another horse and carriage to carry them to Rupert's quiet home in the country. Beatrice and Daniel arrived in the moonlight at the stone cottage, only to find it to be boarded up and vacant of its previous residents. When the carriage stopped, Beatrice turned and looked to the driver suspiciously. Daniel's face bore a genuine expression of surprise that defused any of Beatrice's thoughts of deceit.

"I truly am as vexed and confused of me cousin's absence as ya are."

"I believe you Daniel, but what are we to do now?"

"Tis a bit late to ride back to Manchester."

The couple looked at each other like two schoolchildren on their first date. Daniel climbed from the carriage and walked behind the cottage. He returned with a small board and proceeded to pry off the boards on the front window. He pushed up the sash and climbed inside. Through the veil of shadows, Daniel took a match from the tin to light the oil lamp on the wall. He beckoned Beatrice, now standing on the porch, to join him and helped her through the window. He returned to the carriage to get the basket and the blankets, which he passed inside to her.

"I'll be turnin' the horse out back," Daniel reported. He watered it and gathered an armload of firewood that he found piled neatly in the shed. He prepared the fire while Beatrice unpacked the basket.

"A cup o' tea shall warm ya before we turn in. Please, bring me the corrie, Madame."

Beatrice handed him the kettle, which he filled from the well and placed it on the hook over the fire. He sat down in the rocking chair.

"You are comfortable wi' stayin' the night?"

"Yes, I hope your cousin shan't mind our trespassing."

"Rupert? Nay, he is an easy goin' chap. Cannot imagine where they're off to."

Beatrice sat down in a ladder-back chair next to Daniel.

"Would ya be wantin' the rocker?"

"No, I prefer a nice quiet seat after the ride. Thank you for the ticket, the ride and everything."

"Think nothin' o' it."

Daniel and Beatrice sat before the crackling fire, enveloped in the darkness of the March night. A distant howling broke the peaceful setting.

"Ya hear that?"

"Yes."

"Tis the sounds o' spring. That call o' the red fox shall soon be lost to the whine o' their young." A much louder roar startled the conversing couple.

"The red deer. That must be a rather large one," Beatrice noted.

"You know a bit about nature?"

"A little."

"I fancy meself to be a half-hearted naturalist. The deer are abundant in these parts. That stag probably dons a rack that would cover this wall,"

Daniel pointed above the mantle. Silence soon surrounded the cottage. Daniel rocked and hummed an old Irish tune, while Beatrice watched the flames, mesmerized by Daniel's song. Lulled to sleep, her head slowly dropped, as she drifted off. Daniel soon noticed that his companion had fallen into peaceful slumber, but hesitated in wakening her to retire to the comfort of one of the bedrooms. He examined her face.

Yer a very appealin' woman. Any man would be proud to have ya on his arm. Observing her uncomfortable position, fearing that she may fall from her chair, Daniel gave Beatrice a nudge.

"Time to be retirin' ma'am." Beatrice did not respond. Daniel made one more attempt when he realized that his newfound friend was truly exhausted. He studied her small frame for a minute longer and decided that he would perform the chivalrous task of delivering her to her sleeping quarters.

"All right then," he mumbled after a deep sigh. Daniel left his chair to carry his tired counterpart into the bedroom. Placing his right arm behind her waist and his left beneath her skirted knees, he gently lifted her from the chair and walked slowly and steadily towards the bedroom.

Then it happened. Daniel stopped abruptly when a shooting pain shot up his right leg. He grimaced with the excruciating shock of the cramping sensation. He could not step forward. He fought the tightening of his grasp responding to the unbearable pain. Daniel edged forward, teeth clenched, and his eyes squinting as the cramping intensified. He stopped inside the bedroom doorway to rest and shifted his weight to his good leg to shake out the taut limb. Unsuccessful in his attempt, beads of perspiration formed on his brow and his breathing grew deeper in his desperation to avoid wakening the sleeping passenger.

Daniel looked to the small bed, only a few yards away, which in his despairing state, appeared to be magnified to miles. Daniel closed his eyes and prayed for assistance. He moved forward dragging the bothersome leg, when, to his surprise, the cramping dissipated as they reached the bed.

He bowed his head in gratitude when he caught sight of something disturbingly dark on the coverlet. In the dimly lit room, he found it nearly impossible to determine the nature of the questionable objects. Daniel tightened his grip and squatted slowly, maintaining his balance. There, they were, two black beetles enjoying the comfort of the quilt. *Nay, not tonight!* he thought. At this point, Beatrice's weight had seemingly increased by tenfold in Daniels arms, now weary from the ordeal. Neither hand was available to swat away the invaders. He considered lifting one foot, but realized that this would place his balance in jeopardy. His choices were but two now, neither being desirable. One, he could return her to the rocker, or two, waken her and explain the situation. He chose the second as the journey back seemed impossible. *Not the lad I was,* he lamented, finding Beatrice's minimal weight to be overwhelming.

"Ma'am, wake up," he whispered. No response. "Time to retire," he added a little louder as he jostled her encouragingly.

Beatrice eyes opened slightly, "What?" she murmured.

"Ma'am, I was tryin' not to wake ya, to lay ya in the bed, but there seems to be two belligerent beetles occupyin' it."

"AGH!!! AGH!!!" Beatrice screamed, clutching Daniels neck. "No, please!" she continued in terror.

Daniel, shocked with her reaction, mustered up his last bit of energy and rushed her to the doorway.

"It is alright, ma'am, I meant ya no harm!" Daniel comforted.

"No, no, I hate them!" Beatrice yelled, tightening her grip around his neck.

Daniel sped to the front room.

"You may put me down now I am alright," she assured, gaining control of her breathing.

Daniel, more than happy to oblige, stood her on the floor and unconsciously rubbed his neck.

"Daniel, I am so very sorry. Did I harm you?"

"No, no.... just a wee kink in me neck."

"I hurt you, I apologize. I have absolutely no tolerance for those creatures."

"Not to worry, I'll be disposin' o' them, directly." Daniel entered the bedroom and discovered that the two insidious insects had abandoned their resting spot. He walked over to the door where Beatrice watched. "I shall be closin' the door. We shan't have 'em escape, now." Daniel closed the door and turned back the covers. He checked under the bed, the walls, and the ceiling. Nothing. Frustrated, he sat down on the edge of the bed, pondering the situation. *I shan't be sleepin' in this wee bed, but she'll never agree to take it 'till I find 'em...unless, she thinks I found 'em. Forgive,me Lord, but ya were the one that made me too big for this bed and the floor is not to my likin' tonight.* He stretched a little to relieve his aching body.

"C'mon in, there gone now," Daniel reported with a tinge of guilt.

Beatrice carried her bag into the small guest room with a grateful smile, "Thank you."

"Well, now ya be gettin' a good night's sleep. We shall be leavin' early in the mornin'."

"Goodnight."

"Sleep well."

Daniel retired to the master bedroom. He climbed onto the large feather bed mattress laid back and smiled contentedly at the ceiling, enjoying the nocturnal peace when...

"AGH!"

The next morning Daniel sat up on the front room floor, cold and sore, with every bone in his body seeking revenge. Whereas, Beatrice, on the other hand, rolled over in the large bed in the master bedroom and snuggled down under the covers.

During the meager breakfast, Daniel introduced the subject of their departure.

"I have been thinkin' that wit' few choices as to our destination, it may be for the best, if we continue on to the estate o' me dearest friend. Me sister, is visitin' there."

"Daniel, you do not have to be the good host and guardian any longer. You may leave me in Manchester."

"Now, ya see that would be a wee bit o' a problem. I am not much for travelin' alone these days. Could ya see it in yer heart to accompany me for a little longer?" he smiled pathetically.

Beatrice nodded with a timid grin. The glow of satisfaction brightened Daniel's face.

"Now ya prepare for leavin' I shall be hitchin' up the horse." Daniel climbed out the window and walked to the back pasture where he was surprised to find his horse entertained by a young man perched on the fence rail. Daniel called out to him, "Top o' the mornin', lad."

The young stranger did not respond and continued stroking the face of the appreciative horse. Daniel discerned that the visitor was either deaf or simply ignoring him. He moved closer to make another attempt to be sociable.

"Bonny day, sir?" Again no response. On closer observation, Daniel discovered that the scraggly bearded vagabond carried more than the weight of the soiled coat on his back. The shabbily-dressed soul's unnerving dark gaze took Daniel aback and forewarned him to act with caution.

"Lad, might I assist ya in some way?"

The man stared blankly. Daniel's thoughts began racing through the possibilities. *Would this man be a criminal? Is he on the lam? Is he a thief? Is he a crazed soul, wandering aimlessly?*

Daniel stepped closer, scanning the intruder's body for a weapon, considering the possibility that it may be cleverly concealed. He placed the halter on the horse, keeping one eye on the suspicious character, led the horse back to the gate, and turned to find the man still poised on the rail. Daniel continued to the front of the cottage where he hitched up the horse. Leery of the intruder making off with the carriage, he hurried inside to speak with Beatrice.

"We have a visitor, out in the pasture."

"A deer?"

"*Dear* is a poor choice o' words to describe him."

"Someone?" Beatrice looked with concern.

"A young lad wi' eyes that would haunt the bravest o' men."

"What are we to do? Did he threaten you?"

"No, he did not need words to speak."

"He has a weapon?" Beatrice's eyes widened.

"Not that I can see."

"Then he is probably harmless. Perhaps he is troubled."

"Perhaps, in trouble wi' Scotland Yard."

"That is an irrational assumption, Daniel. The poor lad may need our help."

"He may cut our throats!"

"You have been reading too many murder mysteries. Let me speak with him," Beatrice insisted.

"No! O'r me dead body!"

"Daniel!" Beatrice brushed by him and climbed out the window without any thought to the possible danger ahead.

Daniel followed, "Ya shouldna be doin' this, I tell ya. Wait for me."

Beatrice stopped at the back of the cottage. The young man in his early twenties sat silent on the back step staring out at the empty pasture. She approached him asked, "Young man, have you had breakfast?" Daniel's eyes widened with disapproval and gestured for her to withdraw the offer. Beatrice motioned to the stranger and cheerfully coaxed, "Come on inside."

Daniel rolled his eyes, mumbling as he followed the couple, "Should I go to the woods and invite the wolves to be joinin' us, as well?"

The guest received the meal graciously and ate with proper table manners. Beatrice threw Daniel a victorious grin, but Daniel watched the lad's every move.

"Daniel, may I please speak with you in the bedroom?" Beatrice asked. Daniel scowled at leaving the diner armed with a butter knife, but followed Beatrice to the bedroom.

"Daniel, I realize I am in no position to make any further requests of your kindness, but might we take him with us, if he accepts?"

"I canna believe me ears." Daniel shook his head.

"You know little more about me, than you do this lad. You shared your home and food with me," Beatrice rationalized.

"Ya don't look like him," Daniel muttered.

"He needs us, I am certain of it. We cannot leave him here, can we?" Beatrice pleaded.

"Aye, we can and we shall," Daniel said adamantly.

Beatrice turned away and said with disappointment, "I thought you were different from other men. I thought you were not so quick to judge." The room was silent.

"He rides in the front wi' me where I can be keepin' an eye on him," Daniel replied sternly. Beatrice gave him a grateful hug and hurried in to make the proposal. Daniel shook his head in defeat.

"Sir, if you have no previous engagements, might you accompany us to...?" Beatrice turned to Daniel for his assistance.

Daniel stepped from the guest room, "Scotland."

Beatrice's inviting smile faded. "Scotland?" "More specifically, Lochmoor Glen." Beatrice swallowed and dropped to the chair next to her in a state of shock. The two men looked at the collapsed victim with surprise, then at each other.

Daniel boarded up the cottage window after loading the carriage and helped Beatrice to her seat.

"Time to go, lad," Beatrice said, assured that he would follow. Daniel sat at the reins, anxious to leave, preferably with Beatrice by his side and their newfound adoptee on the road. To Daniel's dismay, the unsavory creature climbed aboard. Daniel snapped the reins and the odd threesome headed toward the Scotland border.

Chapter VI

"Ahab"

"If your name is to live at all,
it is so much more
to have it live in people's hearts
Than only in their brains!"

—Oliver Wendell Holmes

After three quarters of an hour, Daniel annoyed with the stench of the undesirable passenger, drove the carriage off the edge of the road towards a thicket of woods near a stream. He stopped the carriage and suggested that Beatrice remain seated, facing the road.

"C'mon lad, we're goin' for a swim." Daniel snatched a sack from the back and removed a cake of soap, towel, one of his shirts and a pair of trousers. The stranger stared straight ahead. Daniel, whose patience had worn thin with the necessary seating arrangements, grabbed the man's sleeve and gave it a swift yank. "I said c'mon!" Beatrice's eyes snapped closed, praying for Daniel's safety in hearing the bold demands on this quite physically fit young man. The passenger relented and walked willingly down to the stream. He stripped down to his under garments before diving into the chilling water. Daniel tossed him the cake of soap and returned to the carriage. A few minutes later, the odorless young man joined them, placed his rolled clothing on the floor next to his feet and took his seat. Daniel stood next to the carriage and addressed his two passengers.

"Now I want yer attention, the both of ya. Seein' how I am runnin' this crew, I refuse to spend anot'er minute in yer company not knowin' yer names. Since neither one o' ye want to provide that information, I'll be choosin' names for ya meself."

Beatrice pursed her lips to keep from smiling. The stranger displayed his usual indifference.

Daniel looked to Beatrice, "Ma'am, ye remind me of a bonny bluebird, always flittin' about and takin' wing. I shall be callin' ya, Birdy." Beatrice broke into laughter. Daniel smiled, "Ah, ya like it do ya? It suits ya." He turned to his clean companion and looked him over. "I christen ya, *Ahab*."

"From Melville's *Moby Dick*?" Beatrice asked.

"Aye. I would say this lad shall be fightin' his mysterious whale, till he kills it or it gets the best o' him." Ahab never reacted to Daniel's comment. Daniel took the reins and turned to Beatrice. "Birdy, would ya be a bit peckish?"

"Why Daniel, as the naturalist, do you not know that birds eat all the time?" she laughed.

"We'll be stoppin' a few miles up the road to feed ya," Daniel said smiling to her cleverness.

After the relaxing picnic, Daniel reloaded the remaining supplies while Beatrice folded the blanket. Daniel stared up the road contemplating the strange events of the journey, a far cry from his daily routine at the shop. Beatrice broke his train of thought.

"You need not take us all the way to Scotland, Daniel. Ahab and I have taken enough of your time."

"It's been only a couple days and it shall be a pleasant change, returnin' to Lochmoor Glen," Daniel explained.

Beatrice's panic increased with thoughts of encountering Nathan, the abusive husband of her past, and her children. *Lochmoor, I cannot possibly return. Nathan, Grimwald... Naomi, my poor baby girl. Could you be in Lochmoor? Could you possibly forgive me for the lost years? Jeremiah, my son.... There are no excuses, I abandoned you, too.*

Beatrice's somber guilt-ridden face, reflection of her past, alerted Daniel to tread lightly when discussing Lochmoor. "It is late we need to be movin' on."

From their expressions, one would have thought that the traveling trio was departing from a funeral, instead of a picnic. Beatrice sat in the carriage in dread, with thoughts of their destination. Ahab was silent, laden with the weight of some unknown dark secret and the driver lamented the fact that his rescue plan suggested impending doom for the mysterious woman. The only sound in the countryside was the rattling and creaking of the carriage rolling down the road trenched by the spring rain.

One half hour later, Daniel halted the horse, climbed down and walked to the back of the carriage. "Birdy, may I speak wi' ya...privately?" He offered his hand to Beatrice, which she accepted without hesitation. Daniel helped her down from the carriage. The couple walked arm-in-arm down the road. Beatrice's memory of the couple strolling below the flat, came to mind. *If only we could continue like this.* She smiled up at her escort. They turned into the meadow on the left. Ahab raised his brow and smiled, unnoticed. The couple continued walking for several minutes before Daniel stopped and faced her.

"Birdy, I ne'r met anyone quite like ya. I would ne'r intentionally put ya in a discomfortin' situation. I respect ya too much. I understand ya not wantin' to confide in me, but I need to know what yer fears are wi' Lochmoor. I shall protect ya, if I know what 'tis the trouble."

Beatrice examined the freckled face. *Why could I have not met you, years ago?* "Daniel, when I was very young, I lived in Lochmoor Glen."

"I was thinkin' that was the case." *Your resemblance to Naomi may not be a coincidence,* he thought.

"I have both good and ill feelings about returning. There maybe someone there who— this person has connections with the man in London," she said fearfully.

"I understand... we shall face this together, Birdy."

Beatrice's heart warmed with gratitude. She stood on tiptoe and kissed his cheek. Daniel blushed at the gesture. *Could you be Naomi's older sister, a cousin or... Naomi never mentioned her mother.*

He led her back to their troubled companion. The little carriage wobbled off, towards an inn, south of Lochmoor Glen. By dusk the next day, they approached the outskirts of the village. When the Wheaton farm came into view, Daniel slowed the horse in seeing some commotion at the base of the silo. Maryanne Wheaton was holding an infant, accompanied by several small daughters.

"Oh, no, look up there!" Beatrice exclaimed, in seeing a tiny form near the top of the silo. Daniel directed the carriage into the drive. Ahab turned to view the unfolding dilemma. One of the small Wheaton girls had climbed to the top of the silo and was having difficulty returning to the ground.

"Jeanie, hold on!" her mother screamed.

Surprisingly, Ahab jumped from the carriage and ran to Maryanne. Beatrice and Daniel watched with amazement as Ahab ran to the spot beneath the little girl, arms ready to catch her, if she lost her grip. The air went silent. Then Daniel and Beatrice turned to each other in wonder as their once mute companion spoke.

"You are a brave little girl, Jeanie. My name is Ahab, do not be afraid, I am here to help you. Lower your right hand and right foot to the next board beneath you."

She looked down, "Which would be the right,

sir?" the tiny voice trembled.

"The one on the side near your home," he instructed."

"Aye, sir," Jeanie looked to her home as the winds blew her soft blonde hair away from her face. Her mother held her breath, praying for the safety of her third youngest daughter.

Jeanie moved slowly down. "I did it, sir," she announced proudly.

"We never doubted you, Jeanie. You are an excellent climber. You went up safely and you shall come down without any trouble. Go ahead move the left hand and foot now," Ahab coaxed. Beatrice and Daniel smiled proudly, witnessing the unfaltering reassurance which Ahab offered the little girl as she lowered herself, step-by-step, to the safety of his arms. Mrs. Wheaton wept with joy with the return of her daughter. Daniel and Beatrice breathed a sigh of relief and looked on their traveling companion with new respect.

"How can I ever thank ye, sir? Come, share our supper. Bring yer friends," Maryanne insisted.

Noting the poor condition of the farm and the numerous tiny mouths to feed, the three thanked Mrs. Wheaton and excused themselves for a supposed, prior engagement.

"Mum, if yer stayin', shall ye be needin' employment in Lochmoor? Have ye any experience wi' cookin' and cleanin'?" Maryanne inquired.

Beatrice was taken aback by the question, considering her desire to remain in the shadows of Lochmoor society. However, having a ten year history employed with the Landseers in Newcastle, Beatrice nodded in reply.

"The McDonnally's have been lookin' for a charwoman. Since Mr. McDonnally's accident, his wife, Naomi, could be usin' some help," Maryanne suggested. Beatrice's face went white as a sheet. Daniel knew that his suspicions were well-founded, in seeing her response to mention of Naomi. However, Maryanne assumed that Beatrice was fearful of working for members of high society and quickly added, "Or ye could possibly take employment wi' the Stewarts, a couple up the road. They are gettin' on in years and in need o' a charlady. Ye wouldna hae to go into the village; they hae a young boy to run errands for them."

With the discovery of Naomi's presence in Lochmoor, Beatrice made the immediate decision to take up temporary residence in Lochmoor Glen, albeit on the very outskirts of the village.

"Thank you, for your kind interest, Mrs. Wheaton. Daniel, I think that I might stay in Lochmoor for a while. Could you please drive me to the Stewart home?"

Daniel smiled, "Climb aboard." The trio said their farewells to the Wheaton family and proceeded down the road. After a brief introduction, the Stewarts welcomed Beatrice into their home and offered her the position. She accepted and walked out to the carriage with Daniel.

"I shall be stoppin' to make a short visit wi' Abby, then be on me way back to London," Daniel explained. "Would ye be mindin' if I corresponded wi' ye on occasion, Birdy?"

"Of course not, I would be delighted. I shall never forget what you have done for me, Daniel."

He turned his back to Ahab and spoke softly to her, "Me heart has always had a place for a special friend. 'Tis a good feeling to have it filled."

Beatrice fought to conceal her sadness of his departure. Daniel shared her sorrow.

"Do ya enjoy music, Birdy?"

"Oh, yes."

"Perhaps, someday, we can share an evenin' at the opera."

"I look forward to it," Beatrice's eyes filled with tears.

Daniel reached down and squeezed her hand. "Are you certain, that ya want to stay? Will ya be in danger?"

"I have to stay, Daniel. Please do not worry about me."

"Take care o' yerself, Birdy, if ya need anything, me sister, Abigail, is down the road. If she is not available, Eloise Zigmann, me friend's housekeeper would be more than happy to assist ya. Tell her yer a friend of mine."

"I shall miss you, Daniel. Ahab, come visit me if you stay in these parts. Otherwise, take care and I wish you well," Beatrice added, solemnly.

"It has been my pleasure, Miss Birdy."

Beatrice watched forlornly as the carriage, headed toward the home of her only daughter, carrying the most wonderful man she had ever known.

Chapter VII

"The Letter"

"Her life was turning, turning,
In mazes of heat and sound.
But for peace her soul was yearning,
And now peace laps her round."

—Matthew Arnold

That evening, Hiram arrived in London and went directly to his flat, where he found a note wedged under the door. He opened it and stood in momentary shock.

Hiram,

I shall make this brief and get directly to the point. I am truly ashamed of my behavior on our last evening together.

After my encounter with your niece and Mr. Zigmann at the café, I assumed the worst in judging your character and chose to terminate are relationship. Since that day, I have missed you dearly and have been tormented by my rash decision.

Our mutual friend, Daniel O'Leardon, delivered a letter from Mr. Zigmann. It was an explanation as to the nature and foundation of his derogatory comments in regard to your past lifestyle. He was extremely remorseful for influencing my thoughts of your reputation and begs for our forgiveness.

Please accept my humble apologies for dismissing you with such great disrespect. I pray that you shall forgive me and reconsider renewing our relationship. I truly loved Lochmoor Glen and would very much enjoy opening a shop there, as planned. If you find it in your heart to forgive me, I have left flat number eight and currently reside in the quarters above the gallery.

With sincere regards,
Elizabeth Clayton

Hiram folded the paper and shook his head. "Capital. *Thank you*, Mr. Zigmann. You have managed to interfere with my life, once again," he scorned. Hiram unlocked the door, tossed the note on the table and sat down brooding. "Two minutes earlier, my life was in order." He folded his hands. *If I fail to see her and she hears that I have been in town, she may think that I have not forgiven her. If I visit her, she shall believe that I have returned to...* "Seventeen years without a woman and now I have one too many!"

He stormed into the bedroom and removed his shirt. He pulled a fresh one from the bureau, put it on and buttoned it erratically, paying no mind to the improper alignment. Mumbling to himself, he reached for the final button and discovered that there was no buttonhole to accommodate it.

"Blast it!" He began unbuttoning the shirt at a mad rate, resulting in two buttons being hurled across the room. After depositing the uncooperative garment to the floor, he sat down in disgust on the edge of the bed. "I have heard that you give us an exam on occasion to test our moral abilities. But, dear Father, a man can deal with only so much," he complained.

A light knock at the door interrupted his chat with the Almighty. He snatched his jacket and pulled it on over his undershirt. Enroute to the door, his right foot caught on the misfit shirt, which he inadvertently drug along with him. Another light rap stopped him in his tracks.

Great Scott, it may be her! His dark eyes darted helplessly around the room. *What shall I say?* he panicked. *I have not had a chance to review the situation.*

Another rap. He knew that he had no other choice, but to answer the door.

Hiram slowly opened the door.

Just as he had feared, Elizabeth Clayton, potter, stood smiling before him. Her sheepish grin turned to one of curiosity as she inspected his bare neckline. In seeing her focus, Hiram fidgeted with his lapels, "I had only enough time for the jacket," he stammered. "Please, come in, Miss Clayton."

"Thank you," Elizabeth entered the flat with every hope of leaving it on the arm of the Master of McDonnally Manor.

"Please, have a seat," Hiram offered, standing behind a chair. Elizabeth stepped over the renegade shirt strewn across the carpet and took the seat. Hiram's face turned a deep shade of scarlet as he grabbed the shirt and disposed it with a toss into the bedroom.

"How are you, Elizabeth? Would you care for some refreshment?" He stood uneasily, several feet away.

"No thank you. You received my note?"

Hiram looked to the paper on the table and replied, "Aye, I did."

"I think that I should enjoy opening a pottery shop in Lochmoor. It could be the first of many. I could become the 'Kate Cranston' of pottery shops... instead of tearooms," Elizabeth said with as much enthusiasm as she could muster up in seeing Hiram's non-committal expression. Disappointed with his silence, she stood to leave.

"Perhaps, I should be going."

"Please sit for awhile, Elizabeth."

She reluctantly resumed her place. "Hiram, if you can never forgive me, please notify me at once.

I am horribly humiliated, as it is." She lowered her head in remorse. Hiram moved a few steps closer.

"No, no Elizabeth, I am a forgiving man. You have no idea how tolerant I have become."

Elizabeth raised her head with new hope and stood before him. "Very well, then, may we put this entire incident behind us and begin again?"

Hiram stared blankly at her.

Elizabeth withdrew solemnly, "Perhaps not." She turned to walk to the door, and then faced him, "There is another in your life," she said pointedly, "Daniel's sister." Elizabeth kept a firm grip on her emotions, although her regrets for the visit now added sorely to her already wounded pride. She moved swiftly to the door, never turning to encounter the dark eyes that drew her to him from the beginning.

She spoke softly, "That is wonderful for you, I..."

Elizabeth Clayton left the flat for the first and last time.

Hiram stood alone in the parlor in a cloud of disbelief. *It is over. She is gone.* He sat down and unbuttoned his jacket. *What is the saying?*

"'Tis well to be merry and wise, 'tis well to be honest and true; 'tis well to be off with the new love before you are on with the new."

In Stockholm, Sweden, Nathan Mackenzie, Naomi's estranged father, stood at the foot of Vila Ramsey's bed, as she grew weaker with the passing hours. The infection, like her guilt, invaded her frail body and would claim her life within a quarter hour. Sophia's mother, Estelle (Hiram's twin, Hannah) held the near lifeless hand of her abductor and surrogate mother. She watched Vila slip helplessly away.

Despite Estelle's adamant disapproval, Nathan had spent the past fifteen minutes, ruthlessly grilling Vila for information of the whereabouts of a large sum of money. His desperation to find it superseded any past feelings that he once had for the mother of his passed infant daughter. The dilapidated room was dismal and reeked of Vila's approaching death. Now, Estelle waited and watched the mother who she had barely known take her last breaths.

Vila whispered, "I should have taken you back to your mother. I deserved to go to prison."

"I know very little about you, Vila. I have only pity for you. I am grateful for your past confession... I did return home with Sophia, as you suggested. My brother, Hiram, was not there. I thought, then, that I did not belong in Scotland," Estelle explained.

"I am sorry, Este—Hannah," Vila gasped.

Estelle leaned down and whispered in Vila's ear, "I forgive you."

A solitary tear trickled from the corner of Vila's eye as she passed on into the next world.

"Wretched thief!" Nathan smacked the bedpost and left the room.

Hannah McDonnally viewed the quiet body of the woman who had deprived her of a life with her mother and yet, neglected her as a child. She pulled the tattered sheet up over Vila's face and left the room. Ironically, Nathan had paid for Hannah's fare to Sweden in hopes that Vila would confide in her with the information of the money. Unbeknownst to him, Vila provided that coveted information to the two of them, but only Hannah realized it. Hannah's melancholy feelings were soon lost to a deep concern for that revelation and Sophia's involvement with it.

I must go to Sophia.

Hannah rushed off to the lengthy process of making arrangements to journey to her homeland and McDonnally Manor, which involved closing the café and putting it up for sale.

In London, Hiram, aficionado of amorous mishaps shrugged off his despair with the encounter with Miss Clayton and got back on track to his original plan to ask Daniel for his sister's hand in marriage. After several days of business engagements, he prepared to invite Daniel to high tea at the Crystal Cup.

"Tonight, is the night! After a proper request for his permission, I will reveal my plan to take Abigail to beautiful Deeside, after we are married. Aye, the bonny River Dee." Hiram donned a fresh shirt, shaved, polished the dust from his boots and left his flat in a jovial, optimistic mood.

He rapped several times at the door to Daniel's flat before he discovered that his friend was elsewhere. *Where are you, man?* He went down the backstairs and walked around to the storefront. Conrad, from the livery, stopped to speak with the familiar London visitor.

"Evenin', Mr. McDonnally."

"Good evening, Conrad. Have you seen Mr. O'Leardon of late?"

"He left town a few days ago, sir."

"Left town?" Hiram said in surprise.

"Yes, he was in a terrible hurry. Something about a woman...probably his sister."

"Abigail?"

"The Captain said that there was a problem with a man trying to do her harm. I am not clear of the details."

Considering Abigail's assault in the Duncan Ridge woods, Hiram panicked.

"Conrad, I need a fresh pair of horses for my carriage."

"Sorry, sir, I have but one available. It is brilliant under saddle."

"Very well, I shall be back for it within the quarter hour. Thank you, Conrad."

Hiram rushed off to his flat and exchanged his clothes for proper riding attire. He mounted the horse at the livery and shot down the London streets toward the back roads toward Lochmoor Glen.

Meanwhile, Daniel and Ahab arrived at McDonnally Manor. Daniel rapped several times, before Sophia peeked out the sidelight and unlocked the door.

"Uncle Daniel!" She hugged him, and then peered around his large frame for a better view of the handsome passenger, seated in the carriage.

"Hello, Sophie."

Daniel noticed her preoccupation with Ahab and explained, "We traveled from Manchester. I know very little about him. I call him *Ahab*."

Sophia looked suspiciously in Ahab's direction.

"Where is yer uncle, lassie?"

"Why he has gone to London, to visit with you. Abigail has spoken of little else. She thought that he was going to..."

"To where, Sophie?"

"It is of no consequence, now. Should we not ask your friend to join us?" Sophia smiled at the solemn young man.

"It has been a long journey. I think that we shall be puttin' him up in the barn."

"But we have so many rooms," Sophia pleaded, admiring the very appealing guest.

"I think not. Yer uncle would not approve. The barn shall be suitin' him fine."

"Shall I fetch Albert, Daniel?"

"No, I shall take the carriage around and show Ahab his sleepin' quarters." Daniel leaned down to Sophia and whispered, "Ya be keepin' yer distance from him."

The scruffy-bearded Ahab stared curiously at Sophia and smiled at her behind Daniel's back. Sophia pretended that it escaped her notice.

She went back into the mansion and Daniel drove Ahab to the barn, and then returned to the main house to visit with Abigail.

Sophia stood at the window of her bedroom, peering down towards the barn.

Ahab, very intriguing. In fact, you may be the second most handsome man in the world— Uncle Hiram being the first.

She climbed onto the large down mattress and pulled up the thick quilt.

I hope that you are warm enough in that drafty old barn.

Sophia looked to the button-eyed rag doll, the only remnant from her childhood, sitting on the chair next to the bed.

"He *is* quite handsome. I should think that we should get to know each other, very soon. Yes, yes indeed. *Ahab,* hmm? What is your given name?

George? William? James? Horace? Oh, please, not *Horace.* "

Chapter VIII

"The Outing"

"Vessels large
may venture more
But little boats
should keep near shore."

—Benjamin Franklin

The soft April rain tapped at the parlor window of McDonnally Manor. Inside, Sophia sat with Abigail waiting for Daniel, who was to treat them to breakfast in the village before returning to London. Abigail pulled the curtain aside viewing the inclement weather with disgust.

"At the very least, the weather could cooperate. Daniel does not need any further delays in returning to London."

"At the very least, *you* have someone with whom to share your life." Sophia sat on the window seat fidgeting with the bothersome jewel. "Daniel shall speak to Uncle Hiram soon enough and you shall become the mistress of all this," Sophia announced spreading her arms, looking around the room. "I, on the other hand, am destined to the life of a lonely spinster."

"What are you jabbering about?"

"This ring. Ahab shall certainly believe that I am spoken for," Sophia scowled. Abigail looked at her with mocking disappointment.

"Sophia, you should know by now that Ahab is not unlike any other man. The odds of him even noticing the ring, are next to nil, let alone pondering its meaning. If it is such a worry, why are you wearing it, in the first place?"

"Abigail, honestly, do you think that I am an imbecile? I cannot get it off! I have tried everything! I hate this old ring. Its only purpose is to torture me." Sophia examined the ring as though it were a hideous wart.

"If it was in my possession, you could not pay me, to remove it." Abigail examined the ring, "It is spectacular. I want the truth, how did you actually acquire it?" Abigail asked suspiciously.

"As I told you and everyone else, Guillaume

Zigmann gave it to me, as a token of our undying friendship." Sophia threw Abigail an indignant glance.

Abigail fired back, "I might remind you that I was present when your *friend* denied that explanation with every bone in his body. Sophia, the McDonnallys are a proud, honorable clan and you are a member of it."

Sophia scowled and dropped back against the window with the shame of yet another lie.

"Abigail, you have no idea of the manner of chaos which this ring has brought into my life. I have tried everything— greasing, pulling, hot water, cold water, eating less, every possible tactic to remove it!" Sophia left the window seat and began pacing the room, much like her uncle. "It is like a boa constrictor, tightening around me, squeezing the life out of me! I can barely breathe. It is here, twisted around my body, every day, every minute. Very well, I confess; I have lied to everyone....and I betrayed my dear friend, Guillaume." Sophia walked over to Abigail, placed her hands on her shoulders and shook them with each word. "Abigail, I consider myself to be a mature, rational woman, but you have to help me, before it destroys my life!"

Sophia's confidante's eyes widened with the shock of the attack. Abigail took hold of Sophia's wrists and slowly lowered her arms to her sides.

"First, you need to get control of yourself! This is a ring, a piece of jewelry, not Joe Jeannette!"

"Joe Jeanette?"

"He is a renowned boxer who has defeated all of his opponents."

"Abigail, you truly astonish me with your vast knowledge."

"Sophia, if you had a brother who spent his

every waking moment reading *and* you traveled with him for countless hours, you too would be blessed with an archive of information. Now, as for the ring, you need to trust me. I have dealt with far greater challenges than finding a simple solution to separating you from this harmless millstone...I have an idea. First, I need the facts. Sophia, have you done anything...an illegal act in acquiring this ring?" Sophia withdrew, appalled with the insinuation.

"Absolutely not, it was all an innocent mistake, a mistake that I shall probably come to regret the rest of my life! It was that feathered fiend...it is entirely its fault!"

Abigail's tolerance with the subject dropped with each detail of Sophia's lengthy account. She cut Sophia off with a promise to help her, reassuring her that the ring would soon be a mere bad memory.

Daniel arrived several minutes later and escorted them to his carriage parked on the glistening cobblestones.

"I do miss you brother, but please hurry back to London, after breakfast. Hiram may be waiting for you."

"Yes, Daniel, Abigail cannot wait for me to call her Auntie Abigail," Sophia teased.

"Sophia!" Abigail objected.

Abby, I am sorry that me horse cannot sprout wings and fly!" Daniel laughed, snapping the reins.

After their meal together, Daniel excused himself, "'Tis been a pleasure, ladies, but the shop is calling me back to Town, among other matters." He winked at Abigail. "I shall instruct Albert to meet ya at the square in a few hours. Sophia, I also spoke with him about the guest. He shall keep

Ahab busy 'til your uncle returns. Ya keep yer distance and Abby, ya keep an eye open. I feel responsible for bringin' him here."

"Certainly, Daniel," Abigail agreed, smiling at Sophia. Sophia and Abigail expressed their gratitude with hugs and left Daniel to begin their shopping. The two women entered the mercantile and after a brief exchange over the new display of Parisian perfumes, they tested several samples on their wrists. It was not long before they left the area in a cloud of diverse scents and indecision in choosing any of the tempting fragrances. Sophia moved on to the front counter where she waited patiently for Dagmar to return with a carton for Naomi and Edward's wedding gift, the pair of Swedish candlesticks. Dagmar carefully wrapped them while Sophia watched with pride in her selection.

Meanwhile, Abigail meandered through the shelved aisles in search of a wedding present for them, as well. At the front of the store, Abigail lifted a small, jeweled clock from a shelf lined with assorted knickknacks. *Made in Switzerland. Hmm? Delilah.* Abigail's thoughts shifted when she uncomfortably sensed the presence of someone directly behind her and glanced toward the counter where Sophia was watching Dagmar. Abigail's immediate response to turn, was deferred by a low, sinister tone of voice and the breath on the back of her neck

"Later, lassie."

Abigail froze, petrified. Her hands clenched the clock. *No, not again,* she panicked. A second later, the shop door snapped shut behind the departing visitor. Abigail's hands quivered as she tried to regain her composure and return the timepiece to its place. She stared blankly at the clock, and then spun around toward the door. Sophia stepped next to her, grinning with the satisfaction of her purchase.

"Find something, Abigail?"

Abigail slipped passed Sophia and peered anxiously out the window toward the end of the street.

"That slithering snake of a man, how dare he!" She watched the man dressed in black cross the street to the pub.

Sophia questioned her companion's erratic behavior and joined her at the window. "Who?"

Abigail's eyes narrowed with contempt as the culprit from the woods disappeared into the pub. With fear, anger, and that same sickening sense of violation, she turned slowly toward Sophia.

"Abigail, what is troubling you? You are red as a beet!"

Abigail swallowed hard. "Do you have everything?"

"Yes."

"Please, I need to speak with you privately," Abigail steamed with fury. She led Sophia out of the store to the inn where they had dined earlier. "Let us take a table in here." Abigail kept one eye on the pub entry and held the door for Sophia. The two women chose an isolated table at the back of the room.

"Back, so soon lassies?" the innkeeper asked.

"Yes, please, another pot of tea," Abigail requested.

"I shall bring it to ye directly," he announced as he left to the kitchen. Sophia scooted her chair closer to Abigail, whose hands were trembling uncontrollably. "Abigail, what has happened?"

"Sophia, it was that scoundrel!"

"Not the fiend from the woods!" Sophia nearly shouted.

"Please Sophia, keep your voice down. Yes, it was him, that horrid creature who accosted me on Duncan Ridge."

The innkeeper arrived with the tea for which the women thanked him and then continued their conversation.

"Abigail, what did he say?" Sophia demanded.

"Shh...."

"Did he threaten you?" Sophia's voice raised a notch.

"In his usual manner, the same two words," Abigail reported spitefully.

"He said 'later, lassie' again?" Sophia whispered with disbelief.

Abigail gave a quick nod and looked anxiously around the room. Sophia's imagination exploded.

"Who knows when he will strike again? He could seek you out at the mansion and terrorize you on walks! And what will he do? His words could be nothing compared to—"

"Sophia! You are not helping the situation. I feel so disadvantaged. All I know is that he wears black and that disgusts me! I cannot tell you how much that disgusts me— I always preferred men dressed in black!"

"Ah, yes, there is definitely an appealing, mysterious factor to a man dressed in black. Where is he now?"

"He is in the pub. This very minute, that despicable brute is only steps away."

"Abigail, with my uncle and your brother out

of town, I really think that we should report this to Uncle Edward."

"Sophia! Edward? Have you lost your senses! That man cannot keep up with Naomi's dachshund, let alone tackle this...anyway, you have not seen this man— he is enormous! Your uncle and his wheelchair would be an easier target than I am!"

"We have to tell Uncle Hiram and Daniel."

"No, Sophia. My brother is not an aggressive man. I have never seen him raise a finger to anyone. I shall not put him in harms way for my defense. And your *uncle*? Think about it, Sophia, Hiram's hair-trigger temper knows no reason. No, no, Sophia, Hiram was relentless in interrogating me that evening of my first encounter with the villain. I am not about to lose the only man who I ever loved, I shall fight my own battles." Abigail shook her head and sipped her tea.

"You cannot continue to live in terror with his threats or worse."

"I do not intend to."

"What are you planning, Abigail?" Sophia asked skeptically.

"Drink some tea, I have to work out the details." Abigail motioned to the innkeeper, "Sir!"

"Aye, miss?"

"We need to be leaving."

"But, my tea?" Sophia objected.

The innkeeper approached, "Aye, I shall prepare your bill."

Abigail paid for the tea and requested that they leave by way of the back exit. The innkeeper shrugged with confusion, but agreed. With watchful eyes, Abigail led Sophia through the kitchen from the inn, around the corner and down the street to Mr. McDenby's jewelry store.

"'Tis a pity that you have come to think ill of black apparel. Uncle Hiram is absolutely *irresistible* in his black suit," Sophia said with despair.

"That man is going to pay!" Abigail threatened. "But, first things, first. Off with that ring!" She snatched Sophia's hand and pulled her through the door.

"Good day, Mr. McDenby," Abigail greeted sweetly.

"Good day ladies, what would be bringin' ye here this jolly good day?"

"We have a wee request, sir," Abigail explained in her most personable voice. "My dear friend has unfortunately put on a bit of weight, since she accepted this beautiful ring," Abigail held Sophia's hand up for inspection. Sophia frowned in hearing the explanation.

"Now, the poor dear cannot remove it, even to cleanse her hands," Abigail continued.

Sophia reluctantly nodded in agreement. The jeweler left his chair behind the desk and leaned over to observe the ring in question. He held his monocle, lowering his head to get a better view.

"We would be ever so grateful, if you, with your infinite wisdom of fine jewelry, could offer a solution. A small file of sorts, perhaps?" Abigail suggested.

Mr. McDenby moved in closer, peering at the ring, and then looked up at Sophia with severity.

"Where did ye get this ring, miss?" he demanded. Sophia quickly withdrew her hand and plunged into a quicksand of untruths as her friend rolled her eyes with disapproval.

"A... a friend gave it to me, if you must know."

"Who?"

"I do not believe that is any of your concern," Sophia shot back.

"This ring is verra familiar to me and I think that ye would be lyin'!" he shook his finger at her. Sophia drew back from the convicting digit.

"I intend to notify the authorities, straightaway! And what is that yer carryin', more stolen goods?"

Sophia drew the package to her chest. Abigail stepped in between the irate jeweler and her distressed friend.

"Now see here, sir, you are mistaken. This ring resembles any number of designs and she just purchased that wedding gift from the mercantile, only minutes past!"

"Nay, I know me business and I know this ring. It is one o' a kind and the rightful owner spent half o' his life savin's to purchase it for his missus! And I shall be seein' that it is returned to her and ye locked up for theft, miss! This ring is wort' a fortune! I am fetchin' the constable!"

Mr. McDenby pushed passed the two girls to the street calling for help from the local bobby. Sophia turned to Abigail, desperate to escape.

"Follow me," Abigail instructed. They closed the door to the backroom and went directly to the window, which naturally refused to cooperate. After several attempts, it opened and the two fugitives bounded down the alley between the inn and the mercantile.

"Hurry, Sophia!" Abigail warned. They darted through the backdoor to the storeroom of the mercantile with the blaring whistle of the law in the not too far distance. Out of breath, Sophia and Abigail approached Dagmar, busy dusting the shelf below the counter.

"Mrs. MacKenzie, you have to hide me!"

"Vat is wrong, Sophia?"

"I am going to prison! Mr. McDenby has some fool notion that I have stolen this ring!"

The head of the only customer present, rose with this comment.

"Vat? Stolen?" Dagmar asked.

"No, honestly, I swear, I found it!" Sophia confessed.

Harriet Dugan moved swiftly to the chaotic scene at the counter. Her head bobbed from left to right of Dagmar's large stature, trying to get a peek at the ring beyond. Then she saw it.

"The ring! I canna believe me eyes!"

"There she be, the thief!" Mr. McDenby stormed in pointing at Sophia. Abigail did not hesitate to step between the constable and Sophia.

"You obviously are not aware of the identity of this young lady of distinction! This, sir, is a McDonnally, Hiram McDonnally's niece!" Abigail announced.

"And who might you be?" The constable inquired.

"I am the *future—*" Abigail stopped, not wanting to jinx her marriage proposal.

"She is touched in the head and *she* is the thief," Mr. McDenby charged, pointing at Sophia.

"She could be the king's sister and wouldna matter to me— the law makes no allowances for thieves of any social standin'," the constable retorted.

The jeweler grinned with success and was doubly pleased to spot Mrs. Dugan standing behind Dagmar.

"Ah, Mrs. Dugan, is not that ring yers— the one the dark-haired lassie dons on her right hand?"

Sophia cowered in horror. Abigail's eyes widened with the recent implications. Harriet lifted Sophia's hand, damp with perspiration.

"Aye, 'tis a beauty; I had wondered what became o' it."

"I was right on the mark!" Mr. McDenby said haughtily. "This pilferer pinched it from dear Mrs. Dugan! Shame on ye!"

Sophia's worrisome expression grew worse with her lack of defense. Harriet smiled at the glistening stones. Her eyes danced; until they met Sophia's confused and apologetic. She turned to the jeweler, "Yer lad, he is attendin' the new, Glasgow school, is he not?"

Mr. McDenby was confused by the inquiry, but replied proudly, "Aye, he enrolled in the Jordanhill College of Education, this fall past."

"Like it there, does he?" Harriet continued. Sophia and Abigail exchanged curious glances.

"Aye, but I do not—"

"The Kilvert's nephew attends the verra same college," Harriet said shrewdly. "I heard tell that yer son had partaken in a bit of a row wit' his dormitory mate. I believe the constable was called and—"

"Me lad was provoked!"

"Is this not yer ring, Mrs. Dugan?" the constable cut in.

Harriet lowered Sophia's hand, now limp with the shock. Mrs. Dugan said reproachfully, "Ye best be getting' yer facts straight, Mr. McDenby, 'fore ye be accusin' this young lassie o' such treachery! 'Aye, 'twas mine... but me husband, Joseph didna approve of me keepin' it and returned it to the generous customer, who presented it to me."

"Generous customer? And who might that be, Mrs. Dugan?" The jeweler asked skeptically.

"Lucas... the Master of Brachney Hall, ya fool! This lassie's blessed Uncle! Now outta here, the both of ye and stop pesterin' Miss Sophia!"

The two men, mutually surprised, left the shop arguing over the misunderstanding. Sophia stood in wonder, admiring the ring for the first time in weeks and Abigail gave a sigh of relief for the ending to yet one more chaotic event of the morning. Mrs. Dugan patted Sophia's hand.

"Aye, there's not a more bonny hand, than the hand o' youth to don me jewel. Enjoy it lassie. Now, I need to be getting' back to feed Joseph, he has one cantankerous appetite!"

"Thank you, Mrs. Dugan!" Sophia called after her. Mrs. Dugan waved and scurried out the door.

"Vell, dat is dat," Dagmar commented and resumed her dusting task.

"Come along, Sophia," Abigail walked to the front of the store.

"Sorry about the disturbance, Mrs. MacKenzie." Sophia apologized and waved.

"I enjoy a little spice in my life dese days," Dagmar mumbled.

Abigail checked to see if the coast was clear before the two women crossed the street to the green. They found an empty bench behind an oak tree and sat down to collect their thoughts.

"Irresistible?" Abigail pouted.

"Yes, indeed. I think the black curls are definitely an enhancing factor," Sophia added. "However, not to worry, Uncle dons white with nearly as grand an impression."

Abigail, steaming with anger, squinted in the direction of the pub. Sophia spread her fingers of the ringed hand resting on the bench seat. "Uncle Edward gave this to Harriet Dugan? Her customer?"

"Sophia! There he is, hide me!"

"How?"

"Quick, give me your scarf!"

Sophia removed the silk scarf and handed it to her. Abigail tied it over her head, tucking in all the telltale red curls.

"Now, while he is facing the other way, exchange wraps with me!"

"What?"

"Hurry, Sophia!"

They removed their coats and replaced them without delay. Abigail lowered her head and fumbled through her handbag, alluding to an intensive search through the contents.

Sophia whispered, "He is heading in this direction."

"We are leaving. Follow me leisurely. Now," Abigail instructed.

The incognito couple left the bench and began walking in the opposite direction toward the bank. Once around the corner, Sophia stopped and peeked around the edge of the building to check the location of the tormentor.

"He has stopped, to speak with someone, Abigail," Sophia informed.

"Who?"

"You shan't believe it, 'tis the only man with whom my uncle forbade either of us to speak, Ian MacGill."

"Humph, I am not at all surprised."

Sophia took another peek. "They appear to be very well acquainted," she turned and reported, and then resumed the lookout.

"Oh no, they are coming this way!"

Chapter IX

"*Choices*"

"The woods are lovely, dark and deep.
But I have promises to keep,
And miles to go before I sleep.
And miles to go before I sleep."

—Robert Frost

Abigail and Sophia rushed down the alley to a stack of wooden barrels and squatted in the mud behind them. Ian MacGill and the man in black entered the alley and moved toward the barrels. Abigail and Sophia, determined to discover the nature of the ominous association, held their breath, praying that they not be detected.

Ian began, "Tomorrow night, we shall meet at MacKenzie's place."

Dagmar's shop? Sophia thought.

"Ye remember how to get there?"

"Aye, the mansion on the southside of the village.

Grimwald, Sophia affirmed.

"I contacted Cecil, in London. We are to meet him in Norwich. What time, do ye expect MacKenzie?"

"Later tonight. We can ask the Swede, she should know," Ian confirmed.

"He better have information 'bout the loot or his life willna be wort' two shillin's!"

"He said he would get it out o' the nanny, one way or anot'er," Ian affirmed.

Money? Sophia thought. *Nanny…Vila?* Sophia pieced the puzzle together.

"Aye… Now, MacGill, I would be meanin' to ask ye, who would be the fire-headed lassie?"

Abigail clenched Sophia's wrist.

"The Irish beauty?"

"Aye."

"Ye'll get yer hands burned playin' wi' that one. Word is that she is property of McDonnally."

Property! Abigail thought indignantly.

"Which one?" the man in black scoffed.

"Hiram— ye'll meet yer match if ye tangle wi' him," Ian warned with a laugh.

Behind the barrel, Sophia nodded in con-firmation.

"Not even the likes of McDonnally can keep me from that beauty," he brazenly proclaimed.

Both women were mutually appalled in hearing the comment. Then it was silent. Sophia and Abigail clasped hands in a panic, certain that they had been discovered and expecting the worst. But nothing happened. They waited, straining to hear voices, footsteps, anything to acknowledge the presence of the conspirators. Sophia made the move and rose cautiously above the barrels to find that she and her friend were alone in the alley. Abigail followed suit and examined the mud-stained hem of her skirt. Sophia shook off her shoes.

"We have no choice, Abigail— it is our duty. We have to warn Mrs. MacKenzie. She could be caught in the middle of this. She has no one."

Abigail brushed off her skirt and rearranged her curls, "Yes, you are probably right, Sophia. I have to agree with you, those two are undoubtedly thick as thieves."

Sophia threw her friend a questionable glance for the unintentional pun. "This mention of money concerns me. How much time do we have before Albert shall come for us?"

"Now, Sophia...we only have another quarter hour," Abigail said, checking her pendant watch.

"We have time to go to the livery, before we speak with Mrs. MacKenzie. Jake may have additional information about this man."

The two women checked both directions and moved swiftly through the streets to the livery. They found Jake grooming a large black horse. Abigail shuddered, thinking that it may belong to the stranger.

"Good afternoon, Jake," Sophia greeted.

"Hullo, Sophia!"

"How is the bride-to-be?"

"Agnes is well. She's preparin' the cottage wi' me mother." Jake ran the brush over the back of the horse.

"I am certain that it shall be the perfect home for the two of you," Sophia offered.

"Wee, compared to the McDonnally estate, but, 'tis greatly appreciated."

"Oh, I apologize, may I present, my friend, Abigail O'Leardon. Abigail, Jake Kilvert, the postman's son." Jake brushed the hair from his jacket with the same fastidiousness, as his father.

"Miss O'Leardon, a pleasure." Jake nodded.

"Mine, as well," Abigail smiled.

With little time to spare, Sophia began the investigation, "Jake, what do you know about Ian and his relationship with that man in black?"

"I see them speakin' on occasion in strange places. Ye know Ian's reputation; ye had better leave well enough alone, Sophia. He may have served his time, but one shan't trust him."

"Do you know the man's name and his business in the village?" Abigail asked.

"MacGill called him, *Dirth*. He wears nothin' but black."

Abigail shook her head and rolled her eyes.

Jake continued, "No one in the village speaks wit' him. Not verra sociable. He asked for yer name, Miss O'Leardon? He called ye the *lassie at McDonnally Manor*. He asked 'bout Nathan MacKenzie, this week past, too."

Sophia turned to Abigail, "Nathan, Dagmar's husband." She turned and smiled at Jake. "Thank you, Jake. Give my regards to Agnes. We have to be going, now."

"Nice to have met you, Jake," Abigail waved. Jake returned with a nod.

Abigail and Sophia rushed to the mercantile, watching for the reappearance of the two villains. The women arrived to find the door locked and the shade drawn. After apprehensive glances, the women simultaneously headed for the back of the shop. The door was ajar and Sophia entered hastily and called out to Dagmar.

"Mrs. MacKenzie, Mrs. MacKenzie!"

A faint voice from the back room answered, "In here, Sophia."

They hurried in, grateful in finding Dagmar safely restocking the bins of dry goods. They briefly expressed their concern for her well-being and recounted the details of the conversation that they witnessed in the alley.

"Nat'an returning to Grimvald? I vill stay at the Kilverts," Dagmar confirmed without hesitation.

"Perfect," Sophia agreed.

Albert arrived punctually at the square. "Shopping or playing with the pigs?" Albert laughed as he helped the mudpuppies into the carriage.

"'Twas an extraordinary morning, Mr. Zigmann," Abigail explained without further expounding.

"I did purchase the present," Sophia added with minimal enthusiasm. *And I am still wearing the ring.*

On the ride back to McDonnally Manor, Abigail's thoughts of Hiram resurfaced, while Sophia remained caught up in the mystery of the clandestine meeting of the two loathsome men.

Later that afternoon, Sophia stopped by the kitchen to speak with Eloise.

"Mrs. Zigmann, have you seen Abigail?"

"Yes, for a minute. She asked for stationery to write to her brother and returned to the study."

"And Guillaume?"

"He is out strolling with Allison."

Sophia chose a biscuit from the crock on the table, took a bite, and sat down in deep thought. She twisted the flour sack towel that lay before her.

"What are your plans for the remainder of the day, Sophia?"

Sophia looked down at the ring and then the towel. She began wrapping it around her ringed hand. *Perhaps a bandage of an assumed injury…a broken hand? That would hide the ring and Ahab shall take pity on me! Yes, he shall carry my packages and*

"Sophia?"

Sophia snapped back to reality and unwound the towel. "Pardon me; I have a lot on my mind. There *is* an unpleasant task, which demands my attention. I suppose that I shan't put it off any longer. I am not an advocate of procrastination."

"I may not be a procrastinator either, but I never seem to find time to complete all my daily duties."

Sophia smiled at Eloise sympathetically.

"Not to worry, Mrs. Zigmann. I shall insist that my uncle hire an assistant for you," Sophia said cheerily.

Eloise smiled at Sophia's optimism when Rusty ran over to snatch a crumb falling from Sophia's hand.

"Could Rusty use a walk, Mrs. Zigmann?"

"Certainly, I shall fetch his leash; otherwise, he tends to wander. He has taken an interest in the pine martins up at the Dugans' woods." Eloise reappeared with the leather leash and handed it to Sophia. "Make him mind his manners, Sophia. You be a good lad, Rusty."

"We shan't be gone too long. I think we shall walk over to Brachney Hall. Come along, Rusty, do you want to visit Heidi?"

Rusty gave two approving barks at the mention of his canine companion and the two set out through the garden to the back gate. Sophia made a detour to the barn to check on the recent visitor. She poked her head inside the barn door.

"Ahab? Ahab, are you here?"

Sophia found that he was not and continued on to her Uncle Edward's home. Sophia kept a tight grip on the leash as the little dachshund anxiously pulled her toward the edge of the woods. The aromatic delights of the forest floor enticed Rusty to strain every muscle to enter the woods as quickly as possible. The battle between woman and beast continued, once they were beneath the large leafing oaks. Rusty paused every few seconds to explore a new scent.

"All right little man, we shall be here all day! Come along! I cannot bear this any longer, I need to speak with Uncle Edward!" Sophia demanded, walking backward, pulling hard on the taut leash. Rusty stopped head up, and ran full speed towards her.

"Good b—"

The dog ran right past her to the kneeling figure behind her. Sophia turned in surprise and delight to find the handsome, Ahab petting Rusty.

"Ahab, I had no idea that you were here."

The young man did not acknowledge her presence, devoting all of his attention to the friendly pup. Sophia noticed his appealing clean-shaven face, and gathered up her skirt to sit down on a fallen log next to the path.

"He is cute, rascal that he is," Sophia commented, taking her place on the log. Ahab continued to play with Rusty.

Keep yer distance. Daniel's warning echoed in the back of Sophia's mind, the very far back of her mind. "Ahab, would you care to share this log? This is one of my favorite places in Lochmoor. It is usually quite peaceful, but...highly traveled at all times of the day and night," she added with precaution. "It is my, my satiary."

"Sanctuary," Ahab corrected taking a place beside her on the log, bringing countless butterflies to flutter in Sophia's stomach.

Sophia gave him a double take. *You actually spoke.*

"What did you say?"

"Sanctuary," Ahab repeated.

"Of course, *sanctuary*." Sophia sat, not knowing what to say next, an unusual situation for someone who has always been so very vocal. *Perhaps if I tell him something more about myself, he shall feel more at ease.* "Ahab, I have had a rather strange life. Did you know that I am the daughter of the kidnapped McDonnally twin?"

Ahab's brow furrowed.

"I know it sounds bizarre, but my mother is not Estelle Ramsey. Vila Ramsey, the nanny, was, of course, the kidnapper. Mother is uncle Hiram's twin."

Ahab squinted with further confusion.

"She is not here— she is in a café in Paris. He

found her. She sent me here to become a member of the clan...on Burn's Night. Now, I am a full-fledged McDonnally!" she raised her hands joyously. Then remembering the ring, she quickly dropped her arms to her sides and tucked the ringed hand beneath the edge of her skirt. Ahab stared at the animated woman.

"Ahab, I really wish that you would not look at me in that manner," she commanded.

"Do you make a habit of lying?" he asked curiously.

Sophia stood up, outraged, "I beg your pardon? Every word that I have spoken is the absolute truth! I am a McDonnally! We are an honorable clan!"

"Your account is *bizarre* as you say, but I was referring to your longing to have me look at you."

Sophia's jaw dropped with his insolence.

"You, pompous—"

"Have a seat, Miss McDonnally. I shall try to keep my focus on the dog."

Sophia sat down stubbornly, not willingly to sacrifice minutes with the appealing company to restore her pride. Ahab resumed his intolerable silence. Sophia could endure it no longer and asked with little interest.

"Ahab, do you have kin?"

"Were you going to Brachney Hall?"

"Yes, but—"

"Should you not be going?"

"Yes, but there is no urgency."

"That is not what you told your little friend, Miss McDonnally," Ahab murmured in mock reproach.

"You are the most judgmental—" Sophia flew from the log.

"I was only stating a fact." Ahab looked up at her and then to Rusty sniffing a small borough.

"Since you are such an expert on facts, is it not time that you share a few with me?" Sophia demanded. "I want facts! Who are you? Where are you from? Where are you going?"

"If you sit down, I shall tell you."

Sophia smugly resumed her place next to him.

"Your residence in Scotland is one with your approval, Miss McDonnally. Mine is the result of an act of removal."

"You were banished?" Sophia asked astonished. "What on earth have you done? You are not a traitor? Oh, God forbid, not a murd—" She scooted a few inches away from him.

"May I speak?" Ahab fought his agitation of her interruption, without making eye contact.

"Will you please look at me when you are speaking to me?" Sophia commanded.

Ahab raised his brows and turned his head slowly toward her, taxed by her inconsistency.

"Sorry, you may go on," Sophia acquiesced.

"Thank you. I have been banished from my country, a—"

"Which...sorry."

"A very small country in Northern Europe. My father was a financial advisor to the royal court. I grew up in a lavish palace with every luxury. For years, my father performed his duties as a loyal servant until last month. He was executed for embezzlement and I, banished."

Sophia listened intently to the unfolding drama, keeping a respectful distance from the speaker.

"My father was not a thief, but the victim of a

cleverly calculated scheme by the king's daughter. Her goal was to punish me in the worst way for not behaving *favorably* toward her," he spoke with disgust.

"*Favorably?*" Sophia whispered.

"She wanted us to marry. I refused."

"Was she—"

"Beautiful? Breath-taking, but Creazna's heart was cold and made of stone." Ahab left the log and peered down the path toward Brachney Hall. "I was not the only one who found her undesirable, her *parents* found difficulty in tolerating her." He turned to Sophia with softened eyes. "When I failed to meet her demands, without warning, I was put in confinement and my father was put to death, based on a score of lies." Ahab returned to the log. "Perhaps this shall explain my sensitivity to those who do not speak the truth."

"Perhaps," Sophia said skeptically, cocking her head. "Either you are one very clever storyteller of fantastic tales or you are truly a victim of a heinous crime."

"Do you not believe me, Miss McDonnally?"

"Which country and what is your name?" Sophia asked sharply.

"Ah, you do not trust me. In that case," he stood, "I should leave. I shall continue my afternoon walk and leave you to yours."

"Wait!" Sophia shouted as he left the woods.

He stopped and turned.

"Why should I trust you?" she called.

Ahab walked back to her, peered directly down into her inquisitive eyes, and replied, "Why do you hide the ring?"

"Ring?" Sophia panicked and slid her hand behind her back. "Why do you not speak to the others?"

"Why do you not speak of the ring?" He stepped back. "I confessed to you, knowing that our time together may be...excessive. Your knowledge of my past was obligatory."

Excessive? Sophia viewed him suspiciously, torn with being elated that Ahab shared the attraction and disturbed with his openly stating the assumption.

"Miss McDonnally, we *shall* be sharing considerable time together, shall we not?" His soft-spoken words were accompanied with a sincere look of concern for her approval.

Swept away by the handsome stranger's implications, Sophia responded without hesitation, "I believe so."

"Then the choice is yours. Either way, I would prefer that you keep our conversation confidential." His broad smile set her heart racing. He nodded and walked away.

She watched after him in a state of awe. Floating down to earth from the euphoric clouds, Sophia was met with the harsh realization and her self-flogging reprimand. "Sophia McDonnally! You silly, gullible, child! Come along, Rusty, enough of this nonsense!"

On the final trek to Brachney Hall, Sophia's weakness for the gentle face and bold yet charismatic words continued to haunt her. After several raps, she opened the door to her great uncle's home.

"Uncle Edward?"

"In here, Sophia."

She walked to the kitchen.

"Good afternoon, Sophia. So you have been missing your great uncle?"

"Actually, I need to speak to you about a grave matter."

"Sophia? Come sit in the parlor with me," Edward suggested and wheeled down the hall. "What is the trouble, love?"

"Uncle Edward, I have a serious confession to make."

Edward beheld the familiar ring, "I am listening."

"Let me preface my confession with a proclamation of my innocence."

"Very well, proceed," he agreed, covering his smile with his hand.

"I admit that I made a few wrong decisions, but I had no idea they were. *Wrong,* that is."

"In other words, you acted with insufficient knowledge?"

"Spot on! This is the source of my dilemma," Sophia thrust her ringed hand forward."

"Ahh...the ring."

"Uncle Edward, believe me, I had no idea that you purchased it for Mrs. Dugan."

"Neither did I."

"I found it lying on the...ground." Sophia gave her uncle a double take. "What did you say?"

"I, too, must confess, I never bought this ring for Mrs. Dugan."

"Uncle Edward, you need not keep the truth from me, I am a grown woman. I spoke with her today. She said—"

"It was a complex, complicated, mis-construed...it was a misunderstanding, Sophie."

"But, I was nearly arrested, Uncle Edward!"

"Arrested?"

"Mr. McDenby recognized it as Mrs. Dugan's. Abigail and I escaped out the back window and ran to the mercantile pursued by the jeweler and the constable. Mrs. Dugan explained that you gave it to her, but she had to return it. Her husband was apparently upset," she looked dubiously at her uncle.

"They believed her?"

"Yes, or I would be in prison this very minute."

Edward began to laugh.

"It was not amusing, uncle," Sophia scorned.

"I apologize. I was thinking that it is bloomin' phenomenon, how much trouble one little ring can bring to a clan. Harriet Dugan received it purely by accident under the assumption that it was a gift from yours truly. By the way, what were you doing at McDenby's?"

"Abigail thought that he would be able to remove it. It has been stuck on my finger since she arrived."

Edward began chuckling again, "Are you not impressed with this ring, either?"

Sophia looked down at her finger, "I think that it is the most beautiful ring that I have ever seen. Only it has given me a tremendous amount of grief."

"Honestly, you find it appealing?"

"Why certainly. Who could ever possibly refuse it?"

"Oh, I can think of one or two," Edward said with a sigh.

"I have confessed and now, I ask you, what shall I do?"

"It is your choice, Sophia. It is true, it is an extremely valuable piece of jewelry and it seems to have found a home on your hand."

"Again, my *choice*, everyone wants me to

make these life changing decisions," Sophia said with frustration.

"I, for one, feel very comfortable with it on your safe, obstinate finger."

"Do you want me to wear it?" Sophia asked, flabbergasted with the thought.

"I have no one to give it to at this point, with exception to one very beautiful niece who has recently joined the McDonnally clan."

Sophia threw her arms around Edward's neck and smothered his cheeks with kisses.

"Uncle Edward, you are the most generous man in the world, just as Uncle Hiram said."

Edward smiled dimple to dimple.

"That is not all, Miss McDonnally. To help you feel like a proper Scot, Naomi and I have planned a special outing to take you to Ellisland, the farm of Robert Burns. We have to wait until I can trade this chair in for my walking stick."

Sophia hugged her uncle who was enjoying the peace of knowing that the bothersome jewel was, alas, in a favorable place. Sophia was equally pleased that the ring did not affect Ahab's interest in her.

"The day had been a day
of wind and storm;—
The wind was laid,
the storm was overpast,—
Shone the great sun
on the wide Earth at last."

—William J. Bryant

Chapter X

"The Mission"

"A belt of straw and ivy buds
With coral clasps and amber studs
And if these pleasures may thee move
Come live with me and be my love."

—Christopher Marlow

Sophia, bubbling with information of the afternoon encounters to share with Abigail, wasted no time in returning to her home, McDonnally Manor. She entered through the front door to find her Uncle Hiram tenderly addressing her dear friend, wrapped comfortably in his arms.

"Thank God, Abby, you are safe and well." He withdrew his embrace and brought his large hands to cup Abigail's face. Sophia watched, dazed by the romantic scene, as her uncle leaned to kiss Abigail with gentle passion. Sophia let out a sigh of admiration for the touching moment, which gave Hiram cause to withdraw, to investigate the eavesdropper.

"Sophia?" Embarrassed, Hiram straightened his jacket and suggested, "Come, give your favorite uncle a welcoming hug." With one arm dedicated to Abigail, he embraced his niece with the other. "What a grand day, having both my loves here to welcome me."

"Welcome home, Uncle. Did you see Daniel?" Sophia beamed with interest.

"No. Abby tells me that I just missed him."

"'Tis more the pity, Abigail has spoken of nothing else, since your departure," Sophia teased.

"Sophia!" Abigail reprimanded.

"While you two ladies discuss your difference of opinions, I need to get into a fresh suit of clothes. If you will excuse me," Hiram left kisses on their foreheads and headed up the stairs to his room. Sophia tugged on Abigail's hand to follow her to the study.

"Is he not the epitome of all that is brilliant?" Abigail swooned, looking longingly to the stairs.

"Yes, Abigail, he is dashing. Now we have a number of matters to discuss."

Sophia led the star-struck companion through the pocket doors and closed them behind her. She pulled her dreamy-eyed partner to the small, round table and sat down.

"Abigail, I saw him!"

"Edward?"

"No, oh yes, but first I met *Ahab* in the woods!"

"What was my brother thinking, dubbing him *Ahab*?" Distracted, Abigail straightened her skirt.

"Did you not hear what I said?" Sophia prodded.

"You met him in the woods, and..." Abigail urged her on.

"The preliminary phase of our relationship was a bit awkward but he confessed that—" Sophia stopped short, remembering Ahab's request for her discretion. "*That* he desires to spend a great deal of time with me."

"From your expression, I assume that this pleases you. I might remind you, Sophia, that one should proceed with caution. You really know very little about him."

"I know enough to trust him," Sophia declared sharply.

"Ah, so he really is a charmer."

"I would say that his demeanor is as close to royalty as I have experienced. Nearly a prince, I believe," Sophia said with ease.

"And the ring? What did the prince think about your extravagant jewel?" Abigail pointed to the ring on Sophia's hand.

Sophia gave a quick shrug, "It did not interest him in the least. He still wants to pursue our relationship."

"Perhaps, the ring *is* his incentive," Abigail

suggested cautiously.

"What are you insinuating?" Sophia shot back.

"Simply, that the ring is priceless and Ahab is penniless," Abigail smoothed her blouse cuff.

"Do you not think that I am at all appealing to the opposite sex?" Sophia pushed away from the table.

"Of course, you are. You are beautiful, bright, and entertaining. I am only thinking of your welfare. I do not want you to be hurt, Sophia. I am only suggesting that you be on your guard. I would be too, under these circumstances," she added in a motherly tone.

Sophia sat peeved with Abigail's assumptions. Abigail was too content with her own life to continue the battle. "I apologize, Sophia. I do not know this man and I should not judge him." Sophia retreated her defenses, knowing that Abigail's advice *was* worthy of consideration.

"I did see Edward," Sophia changed the subject and moved her chair back up to the table.

"I am proud of you. How did he respond?"

"He was charming, as usual. Are you prepared for this?" Sophia said modestly.

"Prepared for what?"

"He gave it to me," Sophia announced as though she had always expected it.

"He gave you the ring, *Harriet's* ring?" Abigail leaned toward Sophia.

"It was all a mistake."

Abigail ran his finger over the large stone. "A mistake, how so?" she queried with disbelief.

Sophia smiled proudly holding her hand before her. "Harriet accidentally received it through some miscommunication. Is it not gorgeous?"

"Yes, it is. But who was it in—"

Sophia quickly dropped her hand to the table and interrupted; "Now we must get to the plan."

"Plan?" Abigail responded blankly.

"To go to Grimwald tonight, to find out what those two despots are up to," Sophia reiterated impatiently.

"Sophia, I cannot go anywhere tonight. Your Uncle has asked Eloise to prepare a dinner— a *special* dinner for the two of us."

"Tonight is our only opportunity, Abigail," Sophia whined.

"Sophia, not tonight, you have to understand," Abigail pleaded, as Sophia shook her head, feeling betrayed, and left the room. Abigail dropped back in the chair, irritated with the negative connotations made of her anticipated meeting with Hiram.

That evening, Eloise prepared the selected menu for the proper engagement dinner. She followed Hiram's instructions to a "t" and chose a colorful bouquet to serve as the centerpiece. Although she had mixed feelings about Abigail's tactics of the past, Eloise truly wanted her master to find happiness and love. *Abigail O'Leardon, you are Daniel's sister, you have to have some redeeming qualities,* Eloise decided while she placed the silverware.

Hiram, restlessly anticipating the upcoming memorable event, shaved and bathed before donning his finest black suit. Abigail shared his anxious enthusiasm, admiring the new golden dress, which she purchased in London for just such an occasion. She laid it across the bed and began working diligently on fashioning an elegant hairstyle. Sophia knocked gently at the door of

Abigail's room. After identifying herself, she entered at Abigail's invitation, carrying a small plate of pastel fluted sweet sticks.

"I brought a peace offering."

"What is it?"

"Edinburgh rock from Eloise's tray."

Abigail took one of the sweets.

"Sophia McDonnally, you are so terribly naughty; you will spoil my appetite."

"Abigail, I do apologize for being so insensitive earlier."

Abigail finished the sweet and continued placing pins strategically throughout her hair. "No matter, Sophia, 'tis all forgotten. We shall work on the plan tomorrow. Have you eaten?"

"Yes, Eloise prepared my meal in the kitchen. I dare say that you shall be quite impressed with the dining room setting."

"Sophia, tonight I could be dining with your uncle in the mud puddle behind the barrels and not be any less excited."

"Are you going to tell Uncle about that?"

"Absolutely not!"

Sophia spotted the dress on the bed. "Abigail, how posh!"

"I purchased it in London."

"Need any help?"

"No thank you. A little powder and the dress and I am off to the experience of a lifetime!"

"Me, too."

"Hmm?"

"Oh, nothing, I think that I shall enjoy a good book before I turn in, an adventure of sorts."

"Very well, enjoy, Sophia and I shall fill you in on the details in the morning," Abigail giggled.

Sophia returned the schoolgirl grin and left to her room. She closed the door to her bedroom and walked to the window overlooking the grounds. *Perhaps, Guillaume shall go with me. Allison would be a fit to be tied, if we were out scurrying about on a secret mission together...besides, he has not spoken to me, since the card game.*

A soft glow in the barn window caught her eye. *Ahab, of course!* She grabbed her white shawl from the wardrobe, left her room, and hurried quietly down the stairs. To avoid Eloise, preparing the meal in the kitchen, she left the mansion by way of the front entrance. After a full sprint around to the back garden, she rushed through the pasture gate and out to the barn. She cracked open the barn door and called softly, "Ahab, Ahab."

"Come on in, Miss McDonnally."

Sophia slid the door open and found Ahab reading, propped up against a bale.

"Good evening, Ahab."

"Does your uncle know that you are out here?"

"No. I am a grown woman; I do not need his permission to walk the grounds," Sophia countered.

"What brings you here?"

"I need your help." Sophia stepped closer.

"*You* need my help?"

Sophia sat on a bale across from him. "Yes, frankly, you are the only one who can assist me."

Ahab's focus returned to the text and asked innocently, "What shall be my payment?"

"I beg your pardon!" Sophia stood up in disgust.

Ahab laid down the book and leaned toward her, "Money, Miss McDonnally, money. Do you think that I am in the habit of stealing kisses from unwilling young ladies?"

"Ahab, this is a serious matter! This is not a game."

Ahab sat back, "All right. I see that you are troubled. What do you request?"

Sophia gathered her skirt and resumed her place on the bale.

"Ahab, you demanded confidentiality from me. I, too, must insist that you remain silent regarding this meeting and everything that takes place tonight."

"Have you seen me speaking to anyone of late?" he pointed out sarcastically.

"No...but you may," she said doubtfully.

Ahab reached for her hand, "On my honor, I pledge my silence with this kiss." He kissed her hand. Sophia removed her hand from his.

"I suppose that is sufficient," she replied trying not to smile.

"Suppose? Would two be more satisfactory?"

Sophia ignored his comment and explained.

"I am not up to your antics, please listen carefully, we do not have much time. There is a man in the village, Ian MacGill. My uncle despises him and has alluded to the fact that he is a criminal of sorts. Today, when Abigail and I were in the village, we overheard him speaking to the man who..." she leaned forward, "who attacked Abby. They were planning—"

"Wait— attacked Miss O'Leardon?"

"Yes, in the woods on Duncan Ridge."

"Does your uncle know about this?"

"About the attack, yes. About the man's return, no. He took her by surprise at the mercantile. She was in a terrible state."

"You need to report this to your uncle. If you shan't, I shall." He stood up.

"Ahab, you promised!" Sophia left the bale.

"Phia, the man is dangerous!"

"I know, but he is involved in more than his lewd attraction for Abigail. He and Ian are meeting tonight at Grimwald, the property adjoining the back pasture. It was Aunt Naomi's childhood home."

"What concern of yours is this?"

"They are meeting Nathan MacKenzie, Naomi's father."

"Go on."

"Nathan is on the lam for his part in the kidnapping of my mother, when she was an infant. The two men, that I spoke of earlier, were discussing stolen money and obtaining details of it's location from my mother and Vila, the kidnapper. If my mother is involved, I have to know! I have to know if she is in danger," Sophia pleaded.

"We should notify the authorities," Ahab insisted.

"Never! My mother could go to prison. I need information and Abigail needs this man, Dirt or Dirth, whatever his name is, locked up."

"This is not a good idea," Ahab said adamantly.

Sophia faced him, "Very well, I shall go alone!" She turned around and started to leave.

"Phia, stop! I shall go with you," Ahab relented.

She faced him and asked with relief, "You shall?"

"Yes, as I see it, I have but three choices. One, I take you to your uncle and tell him the whole story, after which, you shall never speak to me again. Two, I lock you in a stall until morning to prevent you from going, in which case your uncle shall execute *me*. Third choice: I can risk my neck and go with you. The third is definitely irrational, but more to my liking than the first two. I shall go with one condition."

"What is it?" Sophia asked suspiciously.

"I am in charge of this little expedition; you are to take my instruction. I have experience; I have traveled across Europe and have met every rogue in the business."

"But—"

"It is the only way I shall agree."

"All right," Sophia conceded.

"Now take off that white flag and put this on," he threw her his black sweater. We need to be as inconspicuous as possible." He looked her over. "You wore a skirt, too?" he demanded incredulously.

"Yes," Sophia admitted confused.

"Where do you think that we are going, to the coronation?" Ahab walked back to a crate and lifted out a pair of trousers. "Here, a donation from Guillaume. Go into the stall and put these on."

Sophia held them up to the light. "They shall never fit!"

"Too small?"

"Your humor is not appreciated."

"Whether it is or not, make haste and get in there and change."

Sophia followed his instruction and reappeared shortly, one hand holding her skirt and the other holding up the trousers. A wide grin spread across Ahab's face.

"This shan't do, miss. He pulled a piece of twine from a bale and handed to Sophia. "Belt."

While Sophia added the accessory, Ahab knelt down before her and rolled up the cuffs.

"There, that is much better." He cocked his head and took another piece of twine, took Sophia by the shoulders and spun her around. He gently pulled her hair back and neatly tied it. "Perfect."

"Am I as appealing as the princess?" Sophia joked.

"There is no comparison, you are far more beautiful." Ahab smiled at his accomplishment and entered Hunter's stall.

Sophia spoke up, "What are you doing?"

"Do you want to walk all the way across the pasture?"

"No." Sophia watched Ahab saddle up with a worrisome expression. "He is awfully large, I think that we should probably take Duff," Sophia said insistently.

"The white one? Think, woman! Have you a brain in that pretty head of yours? Why did we abandon the white wrap?" Ahab said with condescension. "Mount up."

Sophia studied the horse, then the bales of hay. She went to the stack and began dragging a bale by the twine tie.

"We need to go, please, mount up."

"I am, I need a little assistance."

"Never mind." He walked over, blew out the lantern, and climbed up in the saddle.

"You cannot leave me!" Sophia retaliated in the darkness.

"Will you be quiet and give me your hand?" Ahab demanded.

"What? I am afraid; I have never been on a horse. Uncle Hiram said that—"

"Enough! If you are coming with me, give me your blasted hand!" Ahab lifted her up behind him. "Now hold on tight around my waist."

"I would rather not," Sophia said, barely gripping his shirt.

"Suit yourself, I warned you!"

Ahab gave Hunter a kick. Without another word, Sophia latched onto Ahab like a steadfast leach. Ahab grimaced with pain as Sophia's nails dug into his torso as they flew into the pasture. He could bear it no longer. He brought Hunter to a halt and scolded his passenger.

"What are you doing? You are going to shred one of the few articles of clothing in my possession and dissect me as well. Please retract the claws."

"Sorry."

"Vedriza mynoud tofmi," he mumbled, shaking his head in disgust.

"I do not approve of profanity."

"Nor do I."

Sophia did not dare ask for a translation. His tone was obviously not indicative of praise for her behavior.

The ride was brief, reaching the stonewall dividing the properties in only a couple of minutes. Ahab dismounted, helped Sophia to the ground and began removing Hunter's tack.

Ahab observed the sky, "The moonlight is a blessing and our worst enemy tonight." He unbuckled the bridle.

"Ahab, what are you doing?"

He snapped the horse on the rump to encourage him back to the barn. "We shan't keep him from his friend Duff any longer. Horses are herd animals, you know. Or do you?" he teased.

Sophia panicked, "Now, how are we to get home."

He pointed to her comical trousers, "Those, my dear lady, are legs, you using them for walking."

"Ahab!"

"Phia, you agreed. I am in charge and we need to be as discreet as possible. This is a wall, not a hitching post. Tying Hunter' legs would have set him into bellowing for Duff. Bright girl that you are, I have to question your reasoning abilities."

"Could we please get going?" Sophia asked snidely, perturbed with his criticism.

Ahab scaled the wall and continued toward the woods. "Have you ever been in these woods, Phia? Phia?" When there was no answer, a moment of panic shot through him. He turned around to find his assistant bobbing up and down, like a jack-in-the-box on the opposite side of the wall. He rolled his eyes and returned to the wall to help her.

"What are you doing?" he whispered.

"What do I appear to be doing?" Sophia snarled.

Ahab jumped the wall and boosted her to the top. He leaped over and reached up to lift her down.

Sophia reached out to him, "Thank y—ahh!"

Ahab jumped back in shock, inadvertently leaving her to fall to the ground.

"Ahab!" Sophia stood up, burning with anger.

"Phia, are you hurt?"

"No, no thanks to you. And why do you call me *Phia*? My name is Sophia. Why did you let me fall?" she demanded brushing off her trousers.

"Why did you shout at me?" Ahab retorted.

"I was not shouting at you, something crawled on me."

"Vedriza mynoud tofmi," he muttered and

grabbed her hand pulling her to the edge of the woods. "Do we have to go through the woods to get to the main house?"

"Perhaps not. There seems to be a road going around it. I hope it leads to the house."

Ahab stopped and took an exasperated stance with his hands planted on his hips.

"Phia—*Sophia* do you not think that it may have been useful to have that information in advance?"

"For a man of few words, you are certainly providing your share. You—"

"Could we please keep our focus on the mission at hand? We shall take the road."

Ahab snatched her hand and they walked for nearly a half mile in silence before the lights of the Grimwald mansion came into view. During their journey, Sophia came to lament her reprimand for the nickname.

"Sorry. You may call me 'Phia'... actually, I prefer it.

Ahab gave no response. A few minutes later, she sought his approval.

"Ahab?" she whispered.

"Hmph?"

"Do you believe that you shall possibly call me 'Phia' again?"

"Maybe."

"Make a decision. Shall you?" She demanded.

He sighed dramatically and leaned over and whispered, "I do not think that I have a choice. If I do not, I shall never hear the end of it."

"Good, you made a decision, not that it matters to me one way or the other."

Ahab shook his head and laughed. Sophia smiled and gave his hand a slight squeeze.

Chapter XI

"The Meeting"

"Love alters not with his brief
hours and weeks,
But bears it out
ev'n to the edge of doom."

—William Shakespeare

Eloise polished the last spoon with the pinkie paper and stepped back to admire her creation. The centerpiece was a stunning arrangement of freshly cut flowers and glowing candles. The damask tablecloth was spread beneath the gleaming china which reflected the dancing flames and the cheerful hues of the bouquet.

With the chiming of the grandfather clock, Hiram left his room to collect his dinner partner. He lifted his fist to tap on Abigail's chamber door. He paused. *The atmosphere has to be exquisite. I had better check.*

Hiram made a quick exit to the stairs and swiftly entered the dining room. His stride came to a halt at the spectacular display before him. Eloise entered behind him carrying a silver tray.

"Mrs. Zigmann, you are to be congratulated. I never envisioned such an elaborate setting. I am truly in a state of awe. I thank you for your delightful contribution to the most important evening of my life." Hiram stepped over and kissed her on the cheek. "I hope Albert shan't object, but no other expression would adequately demonstrate my gratitude," he grinned mischievously.

"Albert shan't deny me every woman's pleasure," Eloise smiled with approval.

"Do not think for one moment that your wages shan't reflect your efforts, either," Hiram assured.

"Thank you, Master McDonnally. Would you care for Albert to play his fiddle?"

"Not this time. Thank you for the kind thought, but I think we shall fill the air with stimulating conversation. Now, I must fetch the beautiful Miss O'Leardon, so she, too, can enjoy this splendid achievement."

"Yes, sir, I shall prepare to serve the soup."

Hiram dashed up the stairs without thought to his undignified sprint and reached Abigail's door half -winded. He rapped lightly.

"You may come in," Abigail invited without hesitation.

Hiram straightened his jacket and entered her room, praying that this evening would end on a more favorable note, than so many of his past dining experiences with her. Abigail stood before him with a sophisticated smile. The lavish golden gown and the jeweled hairpins twinkling in the glow of the candlelit room embellished her natural beauty. Hiram stood, unable to find the words to communicate in his wonderstruck state.

Abigail, on the other hand, shocked to see her escort in the perfectly cut *black* attire, maintained her demeanor. *Yes, you are grand in that suit, but why tonight? I need no reminders of that scoundrel, Dirth.*

However, Hiram's striking features and eloquent speech waived her disapproval.

"Abigail, if I knew not that you were a mere mortal, I would swear by my mother's name that you were the divine representation of all that is perfect and beautiful."

Abigail's face blushed in the glow of his appreciation and she took his arm proudly.

"I thank you, Master McDonnally. Shall we go?"

Hiram quickly reviewed his plans for the rest of the evening while he led her to the stairs and down to the dining room. His evening continued in perfect form with that first moment in which Abigail responded with sheer delight of the magnificent table setting. Hiram offered his future bride a chair, then took his place across from her at the head of the table, some distance away.

"Hiram, everything is lovely! I could not be more pleasantly surprised."

"We have Mrs. Zigmann and her many talents to thank, for this is solely her artwork." Hiram called to the housekeeper waiting to be summoned in the shadows of the hall. "Mrs. Zigmann,"

"Yes, sir," Eloise entered carrying two steaming bowls of leek soup garnished with fresh parsley on a small tray lined with a lace doily.

"Eloise, it is all simply glorious! Thank you." Abigail added.

"The pleasure is mine, Miss O'Leardon," Eloise served the soup, and then retired to the kitchen.

"How did your day fare, Abigail?"

You had to ask. Abigail thought with dread. *There is very little that I dare report.*

"Busy," she answered.

"In what manner?"

"Sophia and I went to the village to get wedding gifts... for Naomi and Edward."

"Did you?"

"Did I what?" Abigail swallowed with panic.

"Find gifts?" Hiram asked.

"Sophia did." Abigail took another sip of her soup.

"What other mischief occupied your visit?"

"Mischief?" Abigail coughed out the word.

"It is a mere expression, Abby," he qualified calmly. "How did you spend the remainder of your day?" Hiram took a spoonful.

"How?" Abigail squirmed uneasily.

"Abigail, I have never found you to be at a loss for words. Is there something troubling you?"

He sat down his spoon. Abigail stared at her inquisitive host and his annoying black apparel.

"The suit," she blurted inadvertently.

"You do not approve of my clothing?" Hiram's heart sank.

"No, no, I adore the suit. It is...it is a piece of lint. There," she pointed.

Hiram helplessly scanned his sleeves, when Abigail left her chair and pretended to remove a stray piece from his shoulder.

"There, now everything is perfect again." Abigail closed her eyes with momentary relief. Hiram escorted her to her chair and returned to his. Fortunately, for Abigail, Eloise arrived to retrieve the soup bowls before the previous inquiry could be reinstated.

Eloise returned with the main entrée. She sat a large, covered pewter charger in front of Abigail and removed the lid. Abigail was aghast.

"Hiram, what is this?" she said fearfully.

"Gigot," he stated with pride.

"Aghh! *Baby sheep*?" Abigail shoved her chair away from the table in horror.

"No!" Hiram explained, "Leg of lamb."

"Hiram McDonnally, I do not eat babies, for you or anyone else!" she stood up with disgust.

"But, Abigail, it is not alive!" He rationalized.

Abigail threw her napkin on the empty plate before her.

"I suppose that you shall want us to live on the Isle of Lewis, so that you can dine on nothing, but babies!"

"Abigail, what are you talking about?"

"Guga, baby solan geese, the delicacy there! You, you carnivore!"

Abigail stormed out of the room in her usual temperamental manner, marching toward the kitchen. Hiram stood up, tossed his napkin and shouted.

"Yes, I am a carnivore! And proud of it!"

Hiram dropped to the chair, landing both tightly clenched fists in a booming thud to the table. Eloise blinked with the crashing of the crystal goblets on to the china plates, but maintained her usual neutral position. Hiram glared at the shattered setting and demanded.

"Eloise, a new plate, please. And serve me."

"Yes, sir," she said meekly and retrieved Abigail's plate and set it before him. She carried over the entrée and handed him the carving utensils.

"Never mind." He grabbed the leg of lamb and took a voracious bite.

Eloise covered her mouth in seeing the primeval gesture.

"I will eat *anything,* in *any* manner I choose," he grumbled.

Eloise nodded and excused herself. *Perhaps, Abigail is not the woman for the master.*

Ahab and Sophia stood at the edge of the Grimwald woods, examining the topography of the grounds.

"What do you think Ahab?"

"Oh, so now you have some interest in my opinion?" he teased.

"Ahab, this is—"

"I know, 'a serious matter'. You continually remind me."

"Ahab, I see movement! There is someone in the mansion."

"Who would have imagined that there would be someone present in a house with a light in nearly every room?"

"Ahab!" Sophia gave him a slight shove.

"Fine, we are going. We can follow that ridge on the other side of the road, and then make our way over to that small shed on the left in the back. Any dogs, Phia?" Ahab gazed across the field to the house.

You did call me Phia. She smiled to herself. "No, I always wanted a cat—"

"On the *property*?" Ahab asked, agitated.

"Oh...no, Flicka is Dagmar's only dog and she went with her to the Kilverts'."

"Good, once we get out back, we can check to see if there is a motorcar or horses. Speaking of which, we do not want to spook the horses. Do you understand?"

"I promise you, Ahab, after we get back I shall repay you for treating me like an infant!"

"Now that you have me shaking in my boots, can we get moving?"

He snatched Sophia's hand and they stole across the road, down into the small gulley. They moved steadily toward the small outbuilding and crept over to hide behind it. The darkness sealed around them with the moon hidden behind a clump of large oaks.

"Three horses," Ahab counted.

"That is an indication that Nathan is here," Sophia confirmed.

"We are fortunate for the cool breeze; they have many of the windows open. I shall check the back entrance in a minute," Ahab whispered and started to leave.

"Wait, we are not going in?" Sophia cringed.

"Only if the opportunity arises."

Sophia gulped, having second thoughts to leaving and abandoning the *plan*.

"Phia, stay close behind me."

Ahab darted to the corner of the house and Sophia shot behind him. With his back to the stones of the mansion wall, Ahab inched stealthily toward the side parlor window. The sound of male voices grew louder.

"Get in there, MacKenzie! We have some things to discuss wit' ye!"

"This is me own house! Ye have no right to be treatin' me in this manner!" Nathan retorted.

Then it was silent. Sophia and Ahab exchanged fearful looks. Ahab cautiously peeked along the side of the window to witness Ian flashing a blade of steel, motioning for Nathan to follow Dirth to the study. Ahab slid back out of sight and gave Sophia a dubious glimpse. Sophia's eyes widened. Ahab gently reached down, grasped her hand, brought it to his lips and kissed it silently. A chill ran through Sophia.

"Dirth, he has it. He is lyin' as good as I am standin' here. He needs a bit more convincin'." Ian twirled his dagger.

"If he's speakin' the truth, that she ne'er spent it, where do ye suppose the wench hid it?" Dirth questioned.

"I tell ye, Vila lived and died a pauper!" Nathan cut in.

Vila died? Sophia thought with surprise.

That is proof he's lyin'. There's not a wench that lived, havin' that much money and ne'er spent it," Ian pulled Nathan close to the blade. "I want me share and now! I did not spend ten years locked up so the likes o' him could live like a king!" The men continued as they led Nathan out. Ian shoved Nathan through the study doorway and down into the desk chair. Ahab and Sophia moved to the back of the house. Ahab checked the door. It was locked, but the kitchen window was cracked open.

"Stay here, I am going to check if the study window is open." Ahab disappeared around the side of the mansion. Sophia stood frozen, trying desperately to convince herself that she was not an infant and that their presence was for the best.

Ahab returned after finding that the voices were muffled and the window closed. Sophia huddled beneath the kitchen window.

"We are going in," Ahab instructed.

"But—"

"We are too close to give up now," Ahab explained, slowly lifting the window. He listened, poked his head inside and climbed through to the floor.

"Come on," Ahab demanded.

Sophia stood on tiptoe and pulled herself up onto the sill. Ahab grabbed her shoulders and pulled her through when a slight snapping sound caught their attention. Both looked to Sophia's *belt*, now in two pieces.

"Oh, no, I must have caught it on a nail," Sophia frowned pointing to a rusty culprit sticking out of the sill. Ahab quickly pulled his suspenders from his shoulders and unbuttoned them.

"Hurry, take my braces," Sophia panicked. Ahab laced them through Sophia's belt loops and tied them in two half hitches. The volume of the angry male voices increased. Ahab pulled Sophia into the pantry behind the curtain.

"Get somethin' to tie him up," Ian called. Heavy footsteps entering the kitchen sent the stowaways' hearts racing. Ahab pushed Sophia down below the bottom shelf and peered out of the dark cavity between the curtains.

"Hmm?" Dirth spied a cake plate on the pie-safe. He pulled off a piece and stuffed it into his mouth.

Ahab's eyes now adjusted to the moonlit pantry by the stream of light pouring through the tiny window. *I need something, a weapon.* He scanned the shelves. The footsteps approached the pantry, Sophia stopped breathing and Ahab reached for a jar of canned cabbage.

The footsteps stopped. Ahab tightened his grip on the jar.

"Aye, a dog leash, that should do the job," Dirth gave a satisfied snarl and walked backed to the study.

Sophia crawled out from under the shelf and flew into Ahab's arms. Ahab was more than happy to oblige with a comforting embrace.

Ahab opened the pantry curtain and stepped out, "All clear," he whispered. "Now, for some of that cake," he walked over to the pie-safe.

"Ahab!" Sophia tugged on his arm.

"Very well, come along, into the room behind the study," he motioned. He raised his finger to his lips, "Quiet, now."

Chapter XII

"Treed"

"And there is even a happiness
That makes the heart afraid."

—Thomas Hood

The thick hall runner muted the young detectives' cautious footsteps. Although apprehensive to the potentially caustic situation, they pressed forward to the room directly behind the study. Once inside the starlit room, the voices of the three men were no longer garbled. Ahab and Sophia stood close to the adjoining wall.

"I tell ye, I dunna hae it! She stole it and gave it away!" Nathan's voice bellowed defiantly.

"What did ye say?" Ian growled.

"Let...let go o' me head," Nathan begged, struggling to speak.

Sophia leaned anxiously toward Ahab anticipating the forthcoming violence.

"Let 'im go, MacGill. Ye hae but one minute, Mackenzie to tell all that ye know," Dirth's low voice threatened.

"The daughter, what did she say?" Ian grumbled impatiently.

"Estelle?" Nathan questioned, short of breath.

"Aye!"

Sophia froze in hearing the inquiry about her mother.

"Nay a word, she knew nothing. She has no money. Her place is but a shambles," Nathan appealed to his captors. Although Nathan spoke only that which Sophia knew to be true, she tightened her lips with the negative comment about the café. "I tell ye, the wench is daft! She ne'er claimed her rights to McDonnally Manor. She has no interest in the money," Nathan continued.

Ahab was met with the realization, *her mother is McDonnally's twin. How could I have doubted her?*

"Ye had two days to get it out o' the Ramsey woman, what did she tell ye?" Dirth shouted in frustration.

"Loosen the leather, yer hurtin' me wrists!" Nathan's pleas were in vain.

Sophia listened eagerly for Nathan's account of the meeting with Vila.

"I... agh!" Nathan groaned in agony.

"More, Mackenzie!" Ian's intimidating voice penetrated the wall.

"I gave her the money to hide in McDonnally Manor. 'Twas a good plan. The law wouldna search there. How was I to know she would make off wi' the McDonnally brat and the money in the middle o' the night?" Nathan paused grimacing at his wrists.

"Get on wi' it MacKenzie!"

"Aghh!" Nathan's boots pressed hard into the floor. "She lived in poverty. She was on her deathbed...she wouldna lie to me— she gave it away, I tell ye, she gave it all away!"

"Who's the bloke that has it?" Dirth snarled.

"Nay, she gave it away to charity," Nathan spit out the words.

"Charity?" Ian scowled.

"Aye, before she passed, she said only one word, 'charity'. I swear," Nathan spoke, near exhaustion.

Sophia's jaw dropped. Her knees buckled and beads of perspiration formed on her palms and her forehead. Ahab, saw her teetering and grabbed her hand, assuming that the scene in the next room was responsible for her trauma.

He whispered, "Phia, get a hold on yourself."

"You fool!" Dirth roared at Nathan.

The sound of several firm punches to Nathan's face further exacerbated Sophia's condition. She was close to hyperventilating when

Ahab put his arm around her and pulled her next to him.

"Shh, my love," he spoke in a calming tone.

Sophia slid her hand across the stubble on Ahab's cheek and pulled his head down with her remaining strength. She whispered in his ear between short breaths.

"I need to get out of here. Help me, Ahab, please." He hastily maneuvered her trembling body to the window. He stood her against the wall.

"Phia, do not move, I shall only be a minute." Ahab released her and carefully eased the sash upward. The creaks of the window were lost in the ongoing dispute in the study. He climbed out the window and coaxed Sophia down. "Now, Phia, come to me."

Sophia weak with nausea, leaned out beneath the panes. Ahab helped her to the ground.

"Can you walk?" Ahab asked.

"I need air." Sophia took several deep breaths.

"We are taking a horse," Ahab said without a second thought.

"No, I shall be fine, but I am not up to a steeplechase," she confessed lightly.

"Are you certain, that you can run."

"I need only another minute. I shall be fine," Sophia insisted.

They sat beneath the window until Ahab helped her to her feet, suggesting that they get as far away from the house as possible.

"We shall head from here to the woods. We dare not go near the road. They may be leaving, as well," Ahab whispered. He led Sophia behind the smokehouse and over to the barn.

"Are you ready to run?" Ahab cupped her

pale face with concern.

"I think that I am."

"You have to be certain; it is a fair distance to the woods."

"I am ready, I shall stay with you."

"Bosiw ed guth."

"What does that mean?"

"May the Almighty assist us." Ahab clasped Sophia's hand and the two sped through the pasture, dodging thickets of underbrush in the moonlight. The second that they entered the woods, the menacing voice called out.

"Stop, trespassers!"

Sophia's heart was racing as fast as her feet. Ahab, breathing hard, stopped and pulled Sophia next to him.

"They have horses, they will certainly catch us."

"Ahab, I am sorry." Sophia's eyes welled up.

"It is too late for regrets. Have you ever climbed a tree?"

"Never," Sophia shook her head, "I grew up in the city."

"You are about to, now. Listen carefully and do what I say. Every second counts. Trust me; I spent my youth in the trees."

"In the castle?" Sophia asked skeptically.

"In the forest, encircling the palace," Ahab replied, losing his patience.

Ahab chose a towering oak, barely visible in the shadows. It was conveniently located next to a smaller under-story variety with lower branches. He climbed to the first set and reached down to her.

"Hurry, they are getting closer. Hang on!" Ahab called, lifting her from the ground. "Now pull yourself up to that next fork. I am right behind you." His thoughts flashed back to Jeanie at the Wheaton farm. "Now, the next one, keep going. Phia, you are a born climber," he urged her upward.

Sophia continued upward with confidence. Ahab was always a branch behind her, guarding her with a watchful eye. The thundering of hooves in the distance sent Sophia to the branch above her.

"Here they come! That is far enough, now straddle the branch, I am coming up behind you."

"Ahab, what if they see us?" Sophia sat unnerved on the large branch near the trunk in his arms.

"Pray that they do not. Pull your feet up and get your balance."

Sophia pulled her legs up, leaning into Ahab's chest for support. She turned her head, moved her mouth close to his ear and spoke softly, "Considering that we may die, I should like to know your name."

Ahab whispered, "Rahzvon, Phia."

"Your surname is *Phia?*" she said with confusion.

He smiled at her with incredulity. "No, *Sierzik.*"

"Oh." *Rahzvon Sierzik. Such a wonderful masculine name...Sophia Sierzik...we cannot possibly die,* she lamented. "Oh, no!"

"What?"

"I forgot to purchase the candles for Naomi and Edward's candlesticks!"

Ahab rolled his eyes. When the pounding hooves stopped at the edge of the woods, Ahab moved his face close to Sophia's and murmured softly, "Leslew zaward skichared."

Sophia turned with questioning eyes, "What did—"

Ahab clamped his hand over Sophia's mouth when the horses moved into the woods.

"Did ye get a good look at 'em?" Ian asked.

"Couple of lads. I dunna like it, they couldna gone far. Ye take this path, I'll take the other," Dirth ordered.

Sophia and Ahab held their breath, sitting perfectly still above the riders. Ahab's protective embrace relaxed Sophia to the point that her foot slipped, etching a piece of bark from the branch to the ground below.

"Over there!" Ian called.

Ahab tightened his grip on Sophia as they leaned toward the trunk. Sophia's heart was pounding so loudly that she was certain that their pursuers would hear it. Ian and Dirth sat on their horses directly beneath them. Sophia's increased shallow breathing, alerted Ahab to put his face next to hers to calm her, when another set of galloping hooves were heard on the cobblestone road. Ian and Dirth snapped their reins to move out of the woods.

"Blast it! Who is that?" Ian cursed. When they reached the clearing he shouted, "Mackenzie! I told ye to tie him!"

"I did! After him!" Dirth shot out through the pasture in hot pursuit to the road with Ian close behind. The treed couple sat silent until all signs of the enemy vanished.

Sophia spoke first, "Aha— Rahzvon, do you think that they shall return?"

"We cannot afford to find out. Do as I say, going down is sometimes more difficult than going up." Rahzvon gave precise instructions for their safe return to earth. They moved rapidly down the path to the edge of the woods facing the McDonnally estate. Together they climbed the iron gate and crossed the road. Rahzvon scaled the stonewall after boosting Sophia over it. He retrieved the abandoned saddle and hoisted it over his shoulder, while Sophia picked up the rug, bridle and reins.

Walking across the estate in the cool night air brought a sense of safety and peace to the bedraggled detectives. Sophia's head was swimming with the details of the Grimwald conversation and the thrill of being held in such high regard by the handsome hero. After the chaos of the evening, the journey back was long and painstaking, but neither party wanted it to end.

"Are you feeling better?" Rahzvon asked, reaching for her hand.

"Yes, thank you... for everything," she felt his protective grip close around her fingers.

"You have been through a great deal tonight?"

"Yes." *More than you know.*

"Stolen money, hmm?" Rahzvon thought aloud.

Yes, stolen money. Sophia shuttered.

When they reached the barn, Rahzvon dropped the saddle and lit the oil lamp on the wall. He heaved the saddle on to the rack. Sophia hung the tack on the appropriate hook and placed the rug in the wooden chest. With a sigh of relief, Rahzvon closed the stall door where Hunter was napping and then sat down on a bale, wiping the sweat from his forehead with his sleeve. Sophia sat down beside him disturbed by her less than appealing attire. Rahzvon looked her over.

"I find it quite to my liking," he said with

conviction.

"Your quarters here?"

"No your evening apparel."

Sophia lowered her head, wishing that she were wearing the beautiful velvet dress that her uncle had purchased for her in London. "How could you, possibly?"

Rahzvon reached over and intertwined his fingers in hers. "Because I am certain that I am the only man in this world who has seen you in such a condition," he smiled.

"I can guarantee that you are," Sophia said uncomfortably.

"I actually feel honored," he added. He reached up and pulled the twine from her hair. Her shiny black curls fell down around her shoulders.

She turned away from his gaze. "I am so embarrassed."

"Phia, you need not be."

Sophia turned to face him. "Rahzvon, what did you mean when you said, "Loo skarch—"

"Leslew zaward skichared." Rahzvon felt her gentle inquisitive eyes searching his soul for an answer. He looked nervously away, unsure and insecure with the deep attachment he had for this near stranger. His mind raced for a creative answer. "I was only commenting that one sometimes prefers to choose one's own candles?" he said with hesitation.

Sophia squinted with a suspicious grin, listening to the pathetic explanation. "Do you also believe that one prefers to choose the proper time—"

He cut her off, "To repay one for treating one like an infant?"

Before Sophia had a chance to respond she found herself wrapped in Ahab's arms experiencing her first real kiss.

"Sophia!"

The startled couple jumped to their feet at the sound of the enraged voice of the Master of McDonnally Manor.

"Uncle Hiram!" Sophia shouted indignantly.

"Get your filthy hands off of my niece and get off of my property before you wish that you had never stepped foot on it! Now!"

Hiram turned to Sophia, "Sophia, I am appalled, Get up to the house and clean yourself up!"

"Uncle, I—"

"*Now*, Sophia!"

Sophia burst into tears and screamed at her uncle, "Vedriza mynoud tofmi!"

Both Hiram and Rahzvon stood in shock at the outburst.

"What!" Hiram demanded.

"Ask him!" Sophia wailed as she fled from the barn. Hiram turned to the intimidated young man. Rahzvon swallowed hard and proceeded nervously to offer an acceptable translation.

"It means—"

"I *know* what it means!" Hiram glared at Rahzvon. Then, Hiram was quiet for another minute, which seemed like eternity for Rahzvon. After accessing the violator, Hiram walked slowly to the wall and removed the lantern. He stepped towards Rahzvon, who was staring fearfully at his opponent, unsure of the irate uncle's next move.

"Come into the light," Hiram abruptly commanded. Rahzvon hesitated, and then stepped closer, eye-to-eye to his accuser. Hiram cocked his head and held the lamp close to the familiar face. "What is your name, lad, your given name?"

"Rahzvon Sierzik."

Hiram's head rose slightly with surprise. "What is your father's name?"

"Gaelon Sierzik," Rahzvon said nervously.

Hiram studied the youthful countenance, pondering his reply. He replaced the lantern. The silence hung over Rahzvon, like the rope of the gallows. Hiram turned to leave and stopped at the door. He spoke sternly, "I shall speak with you in the morning." He left without another word.

Rahzvon remained in the center of the barn with the surprising realization. He stared into the darkness. *He knew my father... as friend or as foe?*

"Forgiveness to the injured
does belong:
But they ne'er pardon,
who have done the wrong."

—John Dryden

Chapter XIII

"Charity"

"He is a fool who thinks
by force or skill
To turn the current
of a woman's will."

—Sir S. Tuke

Sophia stormed up to the house. Her McDonnally stubborn streak took control and she did an about-face, heading back to the barn. Through her blurred vision, the sight of her approaching uncle sent her to duck behind the shrubs in the garden, until he passed. She continued to the barn. She turned the corner to the far side where, to her surprise, she found Abigail sitting on the edge of the well.

"You better go up to the house, Sophia. You heard your uncle," Abigail warned with very little enthusiasm.

Sophia wiped her eyes, "What are you doing here?"

"Your uncle is a cannibal."

"What?" Sophia asked, tired and confused.

"We had a slight difference of opinion."

"I would not doubt that, he is a tyrant," Sophia sniffled, leaning against the barn.

"You should get going, before he discovers that you are missing."

"I have to speak with Ahab. I shan't let him leave." Sophia brushed by Abigail and hurried around to the barn door. Abigail followed. When Sophia came into the light, Abigail gasped and covered her mouth at the sight of Sophia's masculine attire.

"Sophia, what in the world are you wearing? It is no wonder that your uncle was outraged. Are those *his*?" Abigail cast an eye on the barn guest.

Ignoring Abigail, Sophia walked over to him.

"What are you doing?" She asked, watching him pack his belongings.

"Do you realize how many times that question was asked, tonight?" he said bluntly.

"Well? I demand an answer!"

"I am respecting your uncle's wishes."

"How dare you be intimidated, after all that we have been through?"

"This *is* *his* estate and he has the right to decide who resides here." He handed Sophia her skirt. Abigail's eyebrows rose. Sophia folded her arms.

"Spot on! As do I. I am not staying, I am going with you."

Abigail shook her head disparagingly.

"Miss McDonnally, we are from two different worlds," he said sharply.

"Yes, and my uncle should be down on his knees begging for your forgiveness!"

Abigail rolled her eyes with the unlikelihood of that possibility.

Sophia continued, "He may be a McDonnally, but he is not royalty!"

"Nor am I," he stated matter-of-factly.

"You lived in a palace; the king depended on your father!"

"So you really do believe me."

Abigail broke in, "King? Which king?"

"It is of no consequence. As far as your uncle is concerned, I am a worthless rogue. I am grateful for the work and shelter, but now I shall move on, as he wishes."

Sophia appealed to Abigail, "Make him stay!"

Abigail reluctantly sympathized and made a genuine attempt. "Please, stay until morning. Give me the opportunity to speak with Mr. McDonnally. He is not as callous as you may think. You must realize how seeing his niece in your clothing must have affected him."

Sophia clarified the situation proudly, "That was the *least* of his concerns, I am sure. He found us sharing a beautifully intimate moment."

"Intimate?" Abigail repeated anxiously.

"A kiss," Sophia smiled at Rahzvon.

No doubt, that would do it," Abigail shook her head, imagining Hiram's less than charitable reaction.

"Ahab, you cannot let him bully you!" Sophia demanded.

"Stop calling me, *Ahab!* That is not my name!" He heaved the bale of hay next to him across the floor.

Abigail flinched. *Another one with a temper.*

"All right, *Rahzvon,* what about the Lechardee, Wallee?" Sophia pleaded.

A perplexity fell across Abigail's face. Sophia moved in on Rahzvon. "What does it mean? Perhaps I would be a fool to believe you. Has it all been lies? The palace, the disgusting princess, the—" Sophia screamed at him, then started to cry.

Rahzvon threw his head back with aggravation, but could not bear her weeping. "Phia, please stop." He put his arms around her and let out a sigh. *Vedriza mynoud tofmi.*

Abigail observed the volatile relationship, noting that it was not much different from hers with Hiram. *It's the McDonnally element.* Abigail determined.

Sophia continued sobbing.

"Very well, I shall stay until morning," Rahzvon conceded, running his fingers down through her curls. "Now go, before he comes looking for you. Besides, you need to rest."

"Come along, Sophia," Abigail took Sophia's hand.

"You shan't slip away in the night?" Sophia asked wearily.

"I promise, I shall see you tomorrow. You know that I would never lie to you. Now go, before your uncle finds you in here, again."

The two women left the barn and walked toward the house where Hiram watched from the kitchen window. Rahzvon slid the barn door closed and spread the woolen blanket that Mrs. Zigmann had given him, across the strewn hay. He blew out the lamp and stretched out on the makeshift bed. A stream of moonlight through the window narrowed with the cloud cover. He folded his arms behind his head.

Yes, I shall stay, but for how long? That will be his decision. Friend to my father or foe? I should have been more careful, not here in the barn, with her dressed like that. He smiled up at the moon. *She* was *adorable.* He rolled onto his side. *Phia, I hope that I have not severely damaged your relationship with him...* Rahzvon looked out at the mammoth façade of the mansion. "Yes, Miss McDonnally, as impossible as it seems, *leslew zaward skichared.*"

Hiram moved to the parlor and waited impatiently while Sophia and Abigail walked through the garden. The cool night breeze did little to refresh them, as both were preoccupied with their earlier conflicts.

"Sophia, everything shall be fine. You know how stubborn men can be." Sophia turned, wiping her eyes on the sleeve of Rahzvon's sweater.

"Does Uncle Hiram not understand that I love this family and that I would never do anything to intentionally dishonor it? I have been unjustly judged and insulted," Sophia sniffled.

"Sophia, consider his perspective, a male point of view, blinded by narrow-minded suspicions of members of his gender. He *did* find you dressed in what appeared to be Rahzvon's clothing, kissing in the barn when he thought that you were reading in your room. Your uncle has not a single clue to Rahzvon's origin, family or even country. He is naturally leery. 'Outraged' would be more appropriate. Frankly, maybe you should be a bit more cautious."

"I knew that you would agree with him."

"Remember, your family has proven *their* love for you."

And Rahzvon saved my life, Sophia thought.

"Sophia, tell me that you did not go to Grimwald," Abigail inquired with grave concern.

"We did. You can be thankful that you were not there. It made our episode in the village seem like child's play. I cannot discuss it right now. Tomorrow," Sophia promised.

Abigail was not at all satisfied with Sophia's vague report, but honored her wishes to let the subject rest. They met Eloise at the back entry. Eloise ascertained that Sophia was in dire need of assistance.

"I shall draw you a bath, Miss Sophia."

"Thank you, Mrs. Zigmann," Sophia nodded and muttered.

Abigail and Sophia, linked arm-in-arm, continued their stroll towards the parlor. In passing, they were greeted with the fateful voice of the master.

"Abigail, Sophia, come in here, at once."

Abigail nodded to Sophia and the pair stopped and entered to face the suspected wrath. Hiram stood before them, determined to control his anger.

"Abigail, if you would please step into the

study, I would like to speak to Sophia, first."

"As you wish." Abigail released her hold of solidarity from Sophia and gave her a confident smile, suggesting that all would be well.

Hiram began to pace, then turned and addressed her, "You disobeyed me. I told you to go up to the house. Sophia, I am very disappointed in your deplorable behavior, to say the least. You are a McDonnally."

"My apologies, I did not realize that the only place in which members of the McDonnally clan were permitted to show affection, was in the front hall," Sophia said smugly.

Abigail overheard Sophia's remark enroute to the study and cringed, fearing for Sophia's life. Hiram's eyes widened with fury. He walked over to her and loomed over her with contempt.

"I cannot believe that you had the nerve to make that statement!"

Sophia stood tall peering up defiantly, "I am a McDonnally, am I not? We represent all that is good and fair, so I am told. I did not know that there were two sets of rules, one for the women and one for the men!"

"You are here, in my charge."

Sophia held her ground. "I am not a child. I am a grown woman. Would you rather I were spineless, groveling and pathetic?"

"Nay, but you could demonstrate a little discrimination in your choice of the company you entertain!" Examining her clothing with disgust, he added, "And your public attire!"

"I am happy to inform you that *he* liked it," Sophia blurted without thinking.

"That does not astonish me in the slightest," Hiram said disdainfully.

"What are you insinuating?" Sophia scowled.

"I am not obligated to give you any explanations. This is my home and I shall do and say anything that I deem necessary to maintain the reputation of this household and family, miss!"

"If throwing an innocent man to the streets is a sample of the McDonnally clan hospitality, I shan't be associated with it! I would rather spend the rest of my life, scrubbing floors in my mother's café, rather than be associated with such a ruthless..." Sophia broke into tears and fled to the hall and up the stairs to her room. Abigail stepped from the study, observing in silence, as Hiram clenched both fists in the archway, knitting his brows at her.

"Would you like to reprimand *me*, now?" Abigail asked with disapproving resignation. Hiram did not respond. She followed him into the parlor. He sat down in the overstuffed chair and Abigail took the chair across from him.

"Hiram, she is young, but she is not a child."

"She was throwing herself at a man of whom she knows very little! Her proper behavior is mandatory."

"Yes, but she does have a right to her own decisions, Hiram."

"Not if she is living here and is jeopardizing the honor of this family!"

"I agree, Hiram, but before you can expect her to abide by your wishes, you must first have a discussion with her designating your standards. As for Ahab, he may be penniless—"

"His name is Rahzvon," Hiram cut in angrily.

"How is it that everyone knew his name, but me?" Abigail asked with a slighted expression. "As I was saying, his financial status does not necessarily suggest his desire to get his hands on the McDonnally fortune. After all, I could be accused of the same crime," Abigail stated directly.

"Do not compare yourself with *him*."

"Hiram, I shan't, he is much more like *you*."

"Is insolence an epidemic with women these days? Hiram got up and began pacing again. "Perpetrated by the suffrage movement, no doubt."

"I should inform you that, despite Sophia's pleadings, Aha—*Rahzvon* professed that he had too much respect for you and your authority to involve himself with her."

"Fear of my wrath," Hiram walked to the archway, peering up the stairs towards Sophia's room.

"Hiram, he too, is proud and stubborn and was determined to leave. I am certain that he would have, if I had not intervened and explained your caring, generous nature. Yes, he would have left, despite his love for her."

Hiram turned to her. "Love? What does a lad of his age know about love?" he grumbled.

"I here tell that *you* experienced love at even a younger age," Abigail said sharply.

Hiram stopped. His dark eyes pierced hers. He turned away and walked to the window. Abigail followed.

"Hiram, I understand that you adore Sophia and want the very best for her and the family. That young lad has worked hard for you and has asked for nothing."

At least he shares his father's work ethic, Hiram thought. *Gaelon, you were a good man. I will miss our talks.*

"Hiram, you need to trust her. Sophia is an intelligent young woman and shan't do anything foolish." *Except traipse off in the middle of the night with a stranger to spy on criminals,* Abigail's conscience amended.

In spite of her doubts, Abigail continued to support Sophia's case. "She has not lived a life, sheltered from the evils of society."

Hiram took refuge on the window seat with his hands resting on his knees. The room was still, void of the previous commotion, conducive to clearer thinking. Abigail joined him. He flashed back to his encounter with Naomi, months earlier when they shared the window seat. His regrets for losing his temper that afternoon were great; he knew that it could not happen again.

"Hiram, I *love* you." Abigail leaned next to him and kissed his cheek. "Please consider my suggestions."

"I shall speak with him in the morning. If he stays, it will be under strict supervision."

Abigail smiled victoriously, unaware that her input had little impact on the decision, which he made prior to her persuasive speech.

"Good night, Hiram. I do not believe that you are a cannibal."

"At least there is one positive outcome of this evening. Sweet dreams, Abigail." Abigail smiled and left the room.

The portrait of Hiram's father, Geoffrey, further antagonized him, "Save your harsh glare for someone else, Father. You cannot imagine, you never raised a daughter."

Hiram walked through the hall. The tick of the grandfather clock, once again, prompted the memories of those innocent nights and Naomi's sweet kisses. *Aye, I was young and in love, but the fact that he is Gaelon's son, is the only reason that I am being charitable.* He turned to the entrance door, unlatched it and walked outside. The sky was pitch-black with very few visible stars. He sat down on the wall, watching the mist rising on the moors, feeling confused and indecisive.

Upstairs, Sophia lay propped up in her bed, bathed and dressed in the crisp white cotton gown, beneath Rahzvon's sweater. Her dark McDonnally eyes, filled with horror, focused on the rag doll that she held tight in her hands. She whispered to it.

"Charity, could it be true?" She turned the doll over slowly, handling its torso like a poisonous plant.

"Errors, like straws
upon the surface flow;
He who would search for pearls
must dive below."

—John Dryden

Chapter XIV

"The Master"

"No voices in the chambers,
No sound in the hall,
Sleep and oblivion
Reign over all!"

—Henry W. Longfellow

Sophia's face twisted with disgust as she squeezed the Charity's body between her fingers. With her eyes never leaving the doll, Sophia's right hand moved to the little drawer pull in the bedside table. She opened the drawer, felt along the bottom, and removed the small golden scissors. She laid the doll face down and carefully unbuttoned the back of the dress to the "seam". Like a skillful surgeon, Sophia began clipping the stitches down the doll's back. Once the operation was successful, she placed the scissors back in the drawer, closed her eyes momentarily, preparing for the worst. She directed her fingers into the opening and systematically removed small bits of cotton stuffing and placed them on the bed next to her. She paused, and then reached inside. Her fingers fell across the contents and her heart stopped. "Dear God, help me, it is true. I pray thee, help me."

Abigail knocked several times at the door, but received no response. She entered Sophia's bed-room without invitation. "Sophia?" She walked over to the bed strewn with currency. Sophia sat staring blankly at the decimated doll. Abigail stood silent in apparent shock of the unexpected sight, and then reached down to run her fingers through the pile of curled bills, to confirm its reality.

"Sophia, what is all this?"

Sophia looked up with anxious eyes. "It is the stolen money, Abigail. I had it all these years and have never known."

"Stolen? From *where*?" Her heart pounded.

"I do not know. It is the money that Ian and Dirth are seeking," she said in a monotone.

"You are not making sense, Sophia."

"Tonight, at Grimwald, Aha—Rahzvon and I overheard Ian and Dirth interrogating Nathan

MacKenzie. The three of them were obviously involved in a robbery years ago. Nathan got possession of the money and confessed to giving it to Vila, my mother's kidnapper, to hide, here in the house during her employ. She left, without Nathan's knowledge and took my mother and the money with her. At some point, she decided to put it in my mother's doll." Sophia picked up the shell of the doll and dropped it to the bed."

"They know it is in the— was in the doll?" Abigail asked fearfully.

"No, no one knows, only you and I, Abigail."

"You have known, all this time?"

"No, I only discovered it tonight at Grimwald. Nathan kept insisting that Vila gave the money away. He said that Vila said only one word to him on her deathbed, 'charity'."

"I do not understand, Sophia."

Sophia turned the doll over and held it up, "Meet Charity."

"Oh, Sophia, this is a serious situation."

"I know. Giving it to the authorities would reopen the case. My mother and I would become involved. I would have to identify the thieves."

"Yes, that would be extremely dangerous. Sophia, we have to tell your uncle."

"I agree. First thing in the morning," Sophia said as any bearer of ill tidings.

"Sophia, not to worry, your uncle shall know the best procedure in handling this."

Sophia nodded and the two gathered up the large some of money and stuffed it into Sophia's leather handbag with the remnants of the doll. They stowed it in the wardrobe for the night.

"Good night, Sophia."

"Thank you, Abigail."

Abigail gave a concerned smile and left to her room. Sophia ran her fingers down the sleeve of Rahzvon's sweater, and then lifted it to her face. She closed her eyes, drew in a deep breath, and turned toward the window. She folded her hands, "Good night Rahzvon. It is a beautiful name. Please stay. I need you." Sophia closed her eyes. "Dear Lord, please watch over my family and friends... and my dear Rahzvon. I never meant to bring any trouble to them."

The next morning, Eloise left the cottage and entered the garden where she met Rahzvon who was busy weeding.

"Good morning, Mrs. Zigmann."

Eloise stopped with the shock of hearing the mysterious visitor speak. "Good morning, lad."

"When you see Mr. McDonnally, would you please tell him that I shall speak with him as soon as he is available?"

"Certainly." Eloise unlocked the back door and entered the mansion. A drawer and chair lying in the hall next to the parlor entrance caught her eye.

"Not again. Will he ever get that temper under control?" she said annoyed. She hung up her jacket on the hook by the backdoor and began her clean-up duties. Upon reaching the parlor, she gasped at finding furniture strewn around the room, the curtains pulled from the rods and every shelf vacant of the priceless art pieces. Her first thoughts of the damage being the product of her master's ill temper, was foregone, considering the missing treasures.

"We have been robbed, they took it all!" she screamed.

Rahzvon ran in from the garden. Sophia and

Abigail flew down the stairs and joined them in the hall. Everyone stood in shock of the destruction, sharing the discomfort of the violating intrusion.

"Sophia, run up and get your Uncle," Abigail instructed and placed a comforting arm around Eloise. Sophia felt Rahzvon's eyes upon her. Noting her nightdress, she rushed up to her room and snatched her robe. She sped through the hall to her Uncle's quarters and pounded on the door.

"Uncle Hiram, come quickly!" He did not respond. "Uncle Hiram, wake up, it is urgent!" Sophia called. Nothing. Sophia turned the doorknob and peeked inside, "Uncle?" The room was vacant and his bed properly made. A cold empty feeling came over her. Sophia ran back down the stairs.

"Something is wrong, he is not there!"

She found Eloise weeping and Abigail pale and distraught holding a slip of paper. Sophia snatched the ominous piece of parchment from Abigail's limp fingers. Her face was stricken with terror.

"They have taken him," Abigail said tearfully.

"Taken him?" Sophia echoed with anger. "Who?" she demanded.

"Who else?" Abigail scowled.

Sophia turned to Rahzvon in desperation, "We have to find him!"

"We shall and he shall be returned unharmed. I promise," Rahzvon announced with fervent commitment. He left Sophia to Abigail's embrace and fled down the hall through the backdoor. He called to Albert at the woodpile behind the cottage.

"Mr. Zigmann, come *quickly*. Master McDonnally has been kidnapped and they have ransacked the house!" Albert dropped his axe and ran toward the garden.

"There is a ransom note. Tell your son and have everyone meet me at Brachney Hall," Rahzvon instructed and sprinted off to inform Edward.

Albert ran into the cottage and returned with Allison and Guillaume. The three entered the mansion, with the little Rusty trotting close behind, to find the distraught women comforting one another. The dachshund ran straight for the study door and began scratching and barking. Guillaume pulled the doors open. All turned and gasped at the sight of yet another room suffering from the hand of the vandals.

"Outrageous," Guillaume mumbled.

Albert pulled the door closed, "We can all pitch in and clean it up later. Right now, you ladies get dressed. We need to get over to Brachney Hall."

Sophia and Abigail took one last assessment of the rubble and hurried to change. Within a few short minutes, Albert was waiting with the carriage in the drive. All piled into the carriage and headed to Brachney Hall to discuss the dire situation.

"I should have never spoken with him with such disrespect...I love him," Sophia bit her lip to keep from crying. Abigail, empathetic, patted her hand, trying desperately to remain hopeful while also comforting Eloise, now sobbing in her handkerchief. Allison rode, catatonic, silently reviewing her past life with Hiram as "Jack."

At Brachney Hall, they found Edward talking quietly in the dining room with Rahzvon. Edward had calmed down considerably, but was still seeing red. Rahzvon directed his attention to Sophia when she arrived and watched her with concern. She ran to Edward, hugged him, and stoically took her place beside Rahzvon. All gathered around the table and were very surprised when Rahzvon announced, "Before any decisions are made in handling this matter, Sophia and I have pertinent information to share with you." He looked to Sophia to continue. Sophia's initial negative response to his confession gave way to her rational decision to agree with him, knowing that the information would assist in the return of her uncle.

"Last night, Rahzvon, that is his given name, and I visited Grimwald...on a mission," Sophia began. "We overheard Ian MacGill and another man by the name of Dirth, interrogating Nathan MacKenzie. Dagmar was not present; she was staying with the Kilverts. To make a long story short, they were outraged over the misplacement of a large sum of money they had stolen. Nathan, an accomplice, entrusted the money to the McDonnally nanny, who kidnapped my mother. He instructed her to hide it at McDonnally Manor. Rahzvon and I believe that the men, being in the near vicinity are definite suspects in the kidnapping of Uncle Hiram."

Rahzvon suggested, "If we act expeditiously, I do not believe that any harm shall come to Mr. McDonnally. Their interest is money. He is a mere pawn for them."

"Uncle Hiram would be infuriated at being referred to as a only a mere *pawn*," Sophia forced a smile. All in attendance half-smiled with the much-needed humor.

"I think that there is a good possibility that they are holding him at Grimwald," Rahzvon suggested.

"Then let us storm the place!" Eloise jumped from her chair.

"Eloise," Albert shook his head.

"We should at least notify the authorities!" Eloise exclaimed.

"With all due respect, Mrs. Zigmann," Edward cut in, "we need to be very careful and think this through. We need to insure my nephew's safety. Unfortunately, in this wheelchair, I am in no position to be of much assistance. Of course, I have the ransom money, but it is not easily accessible."

"I have money," Sophia spoke up, "a prodigious amount." All regarded her with expected shock, especially Rahzvon whose eyebrows rose instantly with her statement.

Abigail noted the unanimous concern and suggested, "You had better explain, Sophia."

Sophia calmly addressed the questioning faces surrounding her, "I have the stolen money."

"What!" Rahzvon jumped from his chair. "You had the money and you did not tell me?'" he asked furiously.

"I did not know that I had it!" Sophia stood next to him and shouted into his face.

The other members of the group sat astonished with the dialogue.

"You let me risk life and limb, crawling around in trees, facing your uncle's wrath and you had the money all along?" Rahzvon yelled.

"No!" Sophia defended.

"Just what kind of games are you playing? There is a man's life at stake!" he demanded.

"Games! You were the one taking liberties with me in the barn and now you have turned traitor!" Sophia screamed. Ignoring the audience, the incensed couple continued.

"Liberties! You wanted me to kiss you!"

"*I* wanted you to kiss me?" Sophia shouted back.

Seeing the discomfort of the others with the personal nature of the discussion, Abigail stepped in, "This is getting out of hand, now. I think that you two need to go to your corners... sit down!" Rahzvon and Sophia resumed their seated positions, scooting away from each other, as far as the spacing permitted. "Now, I can clear this up for everyone, before anyone gets the wrong idea," Abigail assured.

Abigail clearly explained the story behind Sophia's doll, Charity. Sophia and Rahzvon sat silent, listening, ignoring one another. Sophia began devising a plan during the explanation.

In the Grimwald storm cellar, Hiram sat on the dirt floor, tied and gagged. Dirth hovered over him enjoying his watch.

"The mighty Master McDonnally, eh? Lovely lassie, yer Irish firecracker," he prodded. Hiram's eyes blazed.

"Nearly as tempting in broad daylight, as she was in the woods," Dirth smiled with sinister satisfaction.

Hiram pulled hard against the bindings and biting down on the cloth tight between his teeth.

"Aye, 'twas me that had the pleasure," he ran the blunt side of his dagger across his lips.

Hiram's face broke out in sweat with his fury.

"Nay, shan't be the last time and you canna do anything to prevent it," Dirth taunted.

Hiram's adrenalin surged and his muscles went taut against the ropes when boots sounded on the wooden steps of the cellar behind him. Ian appeared over him.

"How did the grand master enjoy his night? Nasty bump there on yer head," he sneered.

Hiram's burning eyes were fixed on Dirth's.

"Yer kin should be delighted, right 'bout now, wit' the presents we left 'em," Ian mocked. "O' course, they shan't be waitin' too long to prepare the ransom, knowin' that their beloved master's hours are numbered."

Hiram's thoughts skipped randomly, visiting each member of the estate. The threats toward Abigail and how he wish that he could take her in his arms, remorse for his harshness with Sophia, fear for Edward, the gentle Zigmann family and Allison. He closed his eyes. *Please God, guide them and protect them. I will gladly give my life for anyone of them.* His prayer ended amidst the diabolical laughs of his captors.

At Brachney Hall, Sophia presented her plan. "What if *I* were to notify them, that I had the ransom, the stolen money? I could fool them into believing that I was acting on my own accord. Nothing would be more convincing, than the truth about the doll." The others, including Rahzvon, listened with interest.

Sophia expounded, "I would compose a note, pleading for my uncle's release, explaining that my mother had given me the doll "Charity" and its contents. I would offer them the money, in return for my uncle. I would further explain the necessity of leaving the money in the doll for delivery up on Duncan Ridge, so as not to involve the rest of you. I could inform them that I would post it on that large boulder in the field. My supposed naivety would surely convince them." Sophia studied the faces of the rescue group, including Rahzvon's, as they assessed her plan. With a few alterations, they unanimously agreed and prepared to carry it out.

Directly after the meeting, Albert drove Eloise to the Kilvert farm.

"Dagmar, I cannot explain, but it is vital that you stay with the Kilverts for a few more days," Eloise insisted.

Dagmar agreed, "Dat is fine, Eloise. Send vord vhen it is safe for me to return. God be vith you."

Meanwhile, Sophia had Abigail drop her at the edge of the village. She walked to the Tincup, checked her watch and entered the pub. She sat in the designated booth. *Neither, Ian nor Dirth are here. This is the stein.* She placed the rolled note designating the drop off location inside of it without the other patrons noticing. She rushed outside and meandered in and out of shops, working her way back to the opposite end of the square to the alley behind livery.

"Make haste, Sophia!" Abigail called from the cart when Sophia came into view. Sophia climbed up and the two rode off to the manor where they met Albert and Eloise.

During this time, Rahzvon and Guillaume attempted to recover Hiram, before the doll was delivered. The two young men rode Hunter and Duff in unison swiftly down the roads, coming in on the opposite side of the Grimwald estate.

"We will, dismount here," Rahzvon instructed. They abandoned the horses, sending them off to return home. Noticing that there were not any horses tied out back, they snaked their way to the barn.

"Nothing," Guillaume reported. They moved stealthily to the house, listening for any sign of the men.

"We will split up, Zigmann. You check the windows on that side, I will meet you back here." After a thorough surveillance, they met and carefully tried the backdoor. It was open. They crept inside, down the hall, checking every room. They found them empty and void of any evidence to Hiram's capture.

"We should check the other out buildings," Rahzvon suggested. "You check the henhouse, I shall check the smokehouse."

Guillaume nodded. After a few more minutes of futile searching, they met in the middle of the yard reporting no sign of Master McDonnally.

"I was almost certain, that they would have kept him here, Wishful thinking, I suppose," Rahzvon admitted.

"If we fail to find him, the women back home are going to be devastated," Guillaume warned.

"Yes, from what I here, so will most of the women in Britain and Europe," Rahzvon added with a slight smile.

They surveyed the area, then simultaneously announced, "The cellar!" They darted to the storm cellar. The door was locked. Rahzvon ran to the barn and retrieved an iron to pry it open. Seconds later, Guillaume flung open the door and Rahzvon moved cautiously down the steps. Guillaume followed.

"Mr. McDonnally?" Rahzvon whispered in the dark corners. "Nothing down here, Zigmann. A miscalculation on my part," he said with disappointment.

"I suspected the same," Guillaume admitted.

"They have probably moved him. We had better get back to discuss this with the others. We can cut through the woods; it is shorter," Rahzvon said despairingly.

They darted across the pasture to the woods and sprinted down the path through the forest. Rahzvon eyed the memorable oak from the night before and continued behind Guillaume.

When they reached the edge of the woods out of breath, Guillaume asked, panting, "You and Sophia?"

"Yes?" Rahzvon replied bent over trying to get his breath.

"It is obvious that the two of you..." Guillaume hesitated.

"Zigmann, she is impossible...but, I cannot imagine life without her. Unfortunately, after her uncle returns, I shall be moving on, leaving her to the mercy of that sailor."

"Why?" Guillaume took a deep breath.

"Master McDonnally does not approve and I shan't come between Sophia and her love for him. My father always said that a man's greatest treasure is his family."

"Quite honorable, I am not certain that I could be so gallant."

A rustling of leaves, several feet away startled them.

"Probably a rabbit," Guillaume suggested.

Then a moan.

Rahzvon and Guillaume exchanged looks of suspicion, then turned toward the repeated sound and ran to its origin.

"Mr. McDonnally!" Guilluame yelled.

Triumphant smiles pervaded as they lifted the large bound and gagged grateful prisoner to his feet. Rahzvon pulled his knife from its sheath and cut away the gag and ropes.

"Thank you, son," Hiram smiled with relief,

rubbing his rope burned wrists. "Guillaume, I forgive you for all the problems which you have given me in the past.

He patted Hiram's back, "And I you, sir."

Hiram laughed and shook out the kinks in his limbs and addressed Rahzvon. "And as for you, lad, I heard what you said." Hiram looked him straight in the eye. "You, Rahzvon Sierzik, are not going anywhere. McTavish is a fine man and an excellent sailor, but he is not for my Sophia."

Rahzvon extended his hand. "Thank you, sir."

Hiram shook it, "No, I am the indebted one, today. Thank you, men." He dusted off his clothes, "I trust everyone is well, back at the estate?"

"The women are grieved over the ordeal, as expected," Guillaume submitted.

"They are an emotional lot," Hiram smiled, thinking about the comment Rahzvon made about the *other* women being affected by his disappearance.

"If your uncle was not confined to the wheelchair, he too, would be hunting down your captors, this very minute," Rahzvon added.

"Aye, Edward, he may be genteel, but he has the McDonnally temperament," Hiram stretched and placed his arms over the shoulders of his rescue team and started for home.

"Rahzvon, I was very sorry to hear about your father. He was a good friend to me, years ago, when I lived in Switzerland. I owe him. He saved me." Hiram held up his fingers and motioned, "I was this close to becoming Europe's most renowned drunkard."

"His death was a travesty of justice."

"Aye, so I have heard," Hiram gave Rahzvon's shoulder a comforting squeeze.

On the walk back, Hiram explained how he overheard Ian and Dirth discussing the ransom before they left him to rot in the Grimwald Woods. The two young men described Sophia's plan.

"That lassie's a true McDonnally, through and through," Hiram remarked proudly.

When the trio reached the garden, Hiram threw up his arms and yelled, "Hallelujah!"

He flung open the backdoor. In seeing the elated Eloise running towards him, he bellowed, "Eloise, prepare my dinner!"

Edward wheeled from the kitchen to greet his nephew with a comforting hug. Seconds later, Sophia, Abigail and Allison were embracing him, amidst a flood of grateful tears.

Inundated with affection, Hiram announced, "Whoa, Guillaume, Rahzvon, help me out here!"

Guillaume claimed Allison and Rahzvon, seeing Hiram's approving nod, took Sophia in his arms.

"A moment of privacy, please," Hiram keenly announced. He scooped up Abigail and carried her to the parlor. She held tightly around his neck and wept with her face buried in his chest. Hiram sat down on the divan with Abigail on his lap.

"No more tears, love." His fingers caressed her face. Abigail saw the rope burns on his wrists.

"They hurt you," she said, still sobbing.

"Nay, love, this was my own doing, when I met the scoundrel who attacked you in the woods. Abby?" He brushed the back of his hand across her cheek damp with tears. "He claimed that he saw you again," he said gently.

Abigail's conscience balked. *I could not tell you. Dare I now?*

"Abigail? What did he do to you?"

"Hiram, I was frantic when I read the note, explaining that they had taken you. I have not been this worried since...since the fire at the Dugans' when you delayed in coming out of the shed." She tightened her grip around his neck and buried her face in his shoulder.

"Abigail, please look at me." He reached up and turned her chin toward him and demanded, "Why are you not answering me?"

Abigail sat up. "Why does one not answer a question?" she proposed defiantly.

"Because one is harboring some horrible truth?"

"Hiram McDonnally, do you not think that I would tell you if I were to meet up with that wretched excuse for a man?" she scooted off his lap and stood up.

"I would hope that you would feel that you could confide in me, but your hesitation and avoidance of the issue leads me to believe otherwise," he said firmly.

She faced him, "Hiram McDonnally!"

"Aye, that is my name. Did you or did you not encounter this man again?"

Abigail was drawn into his demanding eyes and melted, "Yes!"

"Where did you see him?"

"In Dagmar's shop, on the day that you left for Lon—" Abigail stopped short and closed her eyes, expecting the explosion. Hiram moved directly over her.

"That vermin accosted you again and you did not tell me when I returned?" Hiram shouted.

Those in the kitchen grew silent with his bellow. Rahzvon folded his arms and looked hopelessly at Sophia, who turned away to hide her guilt in the matter.

"Yes, I saw him again in the village! He is horrible and I detest him! Does that satisfy you?" Abigail straightened her dress with a few quick strokes. "Here's the proof! This is the exact reason for not confiding in you— that uncontrollable temper of yours!" she shouted, unconsciously snatching a small vase from the table next to her and smashing it to the floor. The two stared at the debris in shock. In the kitchen, Eloise grimaced.

"*My* temper? That was worth a fortune!" Hiram reprimanded and walked a few steps away.

"It was ugly. I do not know why you are so vexed, you obviously were aware of the encounter or you would not have asked. It appears to be entrapment!" Abigail pointed out.

Hiram turned, "I was not aware that it occurred while I was in Town!" Hiram's blood began to boil.

"Had it happened while you were captive, would it have been more acceptable?" Abigail asked sharply. "Besides, he did nothing. He commented that he intended to see me later, nothing more, nothing less."

"You should have told me, I am not your ward and I am quite capable of making my own decisions! I want him behind bars and this will not happen again! You *will* tell me everything from this point on!"

Abigail thrust her hands to her hips. "Why on earth should I confide in a man who has not even thought to kiss me, after I nearly died of worry over him?"

Hiram stared her down, walking towards her. He stopped only inches away and mumbled, shaking his head, "Vedriza mynoud tofmi."

Abigail scowled. "And what exactly does that mean?"

Hiram said coolly, "Ask Rahzvon."

"Rahzvon?" she clutched his wrist as he started to turn away.

Hiram pulled her close and whispered down to her, "All those hours....I thought that I would never share this moment with you. That pain was greater than the ropes searing my wrists." He ran his fingers through her hair. "Do you want me to kiss you?"

Abigail surrendered to his deep gaze, "Yes."

"Do you promise to confide in me, always?"

"Is this an ultimatum, Mr. McDonnally? she said coyly.

"A kiss for a promise? Surely you would not deny a man who was only seconds from death, a moment of true happiness with the most beautiful—"

"And intelligent," Abigail added.

"And intelligent woman in the world?"

"It could be construed as selfish, I suppose," Abigail hesitated.

"Aye and foolish. Not an intelligent decision on your part."

"And pray tell, why might that be?"

"Because you would be denying yourself your greatest desire."

"I must confess and confide in you that you are you are accurate in your evaluation."

As their lips met, Hiram pulled back.

"Do you promise, Miss O'Leardon?"

"Aye, Mr. McDonnally. Welcome home."

Chapter XV

"The Plan"

"And now abideth faith,
hope, charity, these three;
but the greatest of these is charity."

—St. Paul

The couple indulged in several minutes in becoming reacquainted before they joined the others at the dining room table to enjoy Eloise's fine food. With their return, the other guests discarded any notion of the two separating.

Hiram ate heartily and insisted that the Zigmann's share the table with them. Between bites, he recounted his experience of the evening past, during which his attackers knocked him unconscious in the portal. Likewise, Sophia and Rahzvon confessed to their visit to Grimwald, of which Hiram voiced his disapproval, but acknowledged his good fortune in that their venture aided his discovery.

The remainder of the meal was spent in discussing the second part of the plan to capture Ian and Dirth. Nathan MacKenzie was no longer an issue, as word was that once again, he had fled Lochmoor Glen.

"Guillaume, I need you to solicit the advice of Joseph Dugan in procuring a large fishing net, tomorrow morning. Explain that it is urgent and he will be paid for his time. If you could accompany him to the harbor to retrieve it, I would appreciate it. I dare not leave the estate until the last minute to avoid being seen."

"I understand, Mr. McDonnally."

The next morning, Guillaume and Joseph left the village to meet with Joseph's old shipmate. The cool brackish breeze and the smell of fish, coupled with the sound of the boats knocking rhythmically against the pilings, greeted them as they hurried to the northern end of the dock. They passed the fish gutters, out in full force, working diligently in pools of fish scales. Guillaume did his best to keep up with Joseph, who managed a challenging pace in spite of his arthritic limp. When they reached their destination, Joseph hobbled down the short pier.

"Sharkface!" he called.

A white bearded, husky man with a mouthful of snaggled teeth arrived portside. Guillaume immediately lost all doubt to the sailor's nickname.

"Twigman, me ol' mate! C'mon aboard!"

Guillaume followed Joseph onto the trawler, taking care to maintain his balance. The sailor finished tying the last two knots in repairing a large net, spread out on the deck.

"I will be needin' a net for a day, not near as large as this one," Joseph explained.

"Back in the business o' fishin', matey?"

"Ye might say that."

"Aye?"

"I will be returnin' it back in good order in a couple o' days," Joseph assured. "This here is the son o' me neighbor, Albert."

Guillaume gave a casual salute. Sharkface raised his brows and led them to a large wooden crate.

"This will work for ye," he pulled out a bundled net and handed it to Joseph, who in turn handed it to Guillaume, whose face reddened under the strain of the weight. Joseph and Sharkface chuckled at the sight of the lanky Zigmann's knees buckling.

"Hand it o'r, lad." Joseph's massive arms relieved Guillaume of the burden. "Prepare yerself for a steak dinner, when I return!" Joseph said gratefully to Sharkface.

"Aye, me mouth is waterin' already!" the sailor waved and returned to his work.

Joseph and his embarrassed attendant walked back to the cart. Joseph tossed the net into the back and threw a tarpaulin over it when a familiar voice could be heard calling in the distance.

"Mr. Dugan! Mr. Dugan!"

Guillaume and Joseph turned to see the exuberant, tanned face of Henry McTavish.

"Tavy, me lad!" Joseph gave a powerful embrace to the young sailor.

Henry turned to Guillaume and offered a firm handshake, "Zigmann, good to see ye!"

"Tavy." Guillaume forced a smile and accepted.

"Come to fetch me, did ye?" Tavy asked beaming.

"Ye in for awhile?" Joseph asked eagerly.

"Aye, how is Ma Dugan?"

"Ornery as ever, ye'll see for yerself. Hop in."

Henry threw a small satchel with his personal belongings into the back and climbed up on the seat next to Joseph.

"Get aboard, Guillaume," Joseph called.

Guillaume, leery of Tavy's return, retired to the only available place, in the back, next to the net. Shortly after they began the trip back to McDonnally Manor, Tavy leaned back and yelled to Guillaume, "What became o' the sweet lassie at the manor?"

Guillaume, incensed and his self-confidence wavering, glared, at his muscular peer, who once had eyes for Allison.

Tavy turned back for a reply when he noticed Guillaume's negative response.

"Nay, not the lovely Miss O'Connor, the black haired beauty, McDonnally's niece?"

"Sophia?" Guillaume asked with relief.

"Aye!"

"She is there," Guillaume reported.

"'Tis the best news o' the day!" Tavy smiled ear-to-ear and faced forward.

Guillaume leaned against the seat, satisfied, knowing that Tavy had no designs on Allison. However, he doubted his interests in Sophia would be appreciated by Rahzvon. Joseph drove the cart into the McDonnally barn, unloaded the net and pulled out to leave. As they exited, Guillaume thanked Joseph and told Tavy that he would meet with him later.

Tavy called out, "Zigmann, tell Sophia I shall be callin' verra soon!"

Rahzvon stood outside the barn door. He scrutinized Joseph's passenger as the Dugan cart pulled away and walked into the barn where Guillaume was untangling the net.

"How long is he stayin?" Rahzvon inquired casually.

"Probably not long, his shore leave is usually brief."

"Sailor?" Rahzvon pondered his competition.

"Yes, indeed."

The disturbing vision of the expensive ring on Sophia's finger flashed in Rahzvon's memory. "Has he money?"

"I suppose, he brings in a fair sum. He buys gifts for the Dugans. They have adopted him, so to speak; he has no kin." Guillaume began refolding the net. "His father was Mr. Dugan's shipmate."

Rahzvon helped fold up the net, "So he visits Lochmoor often?"

Guillaume could see the wheels turning in Rahzvon's jealous head. "As often as time permits."

At quarter past ten that morning, the components for the plan were nearly ready, with one miscalculated exception. Eloise entered the parlor carrying a floral dress and matching bonnet.

"This should do very well." Eloise handed it to Rahzvon. He held it up for examination. Sophia joined him and placed the sleeve over his arm. She studied his muscular forearms and smiled timidly. Her eyes scanned Rahzvon's large frame, nervously trying to conceal her attraction.

She sighed, smiled and said simply, "I think not."

Abigail giggled, "I think you are right, Sophia. It will be like stuffing a hay bale into a bread box!"

Eloise spoke up, "But, I have none that are larger and we do not have time to alter it."

Sophia cut in, "He cannot pose as me dressed like that, so I shall have to go myself."

"Absolutely not!" Rahzvon's disapproval echoed throughout the room. Everyone became quiet with his unexpected response until Hiram spoke.

"I agree with Rahzvon. Sophia, we are not taking that chance."

"What are we to do?" Eloise asked.

All eyes fell on Guillaume, resting comfortably in the rocking chair.

"Oh, no, not me," Guillaume whined.

"Son, you are the only man that can where this," Eloise pulled the dress over his head. It fit with room to spare.

"Stand up and be counted, you proud ...bread crumb!" Abigail laughed. Guillaume smiled and delighted the applauding group with a humorous curtsey.

"Now son, you know that I would not support your going, if I did not believe you to be an excellent rider," Eloise explained.

"Aye, he is an excellent horseman, I would wager his abilities against any man in Scotland," Hiram offered encouragingly.

Eloise tied the bonnet tight under her son's chin, and to Guillaume's dismay, commented as to satisfying her curiosity to a daughter's countenance. She double tied the bow, knowing that losing the bonnet may mean losing her son. "Sophia, could you please help him with the buttons, Abigail and I have to get to work on the doll."

"My pleasure." Sophia began buttoning the back of the dress while Rahzvon watched from across the room. Guillaume found the entire scene demeaning, but realized that it was all in the line of duty.

Abigail and Eloise stuffed Charity with parchment paper, placing several large bills on top before stitching up the seam, She was busy tying the back bow when Guillaume announced, out of the blue, "McTavish is back."

"When did he arrive?" Allison asked enthusiastically. Guillaume was annoyed in that his girl was the first to respond.

"Today, Mr. Dugan and I picked him up at the wharf."

Rahzvon kept a keen eye on Sophia, watching her reaction to the news.

Lost in her thoughts of the plan, Sophia straightened the bow, her head cocked curiously, "Did you say Tavy is in Lochmoor?"

Guillaume looked to Rahzvon, then to Sophia, questioning whether to relay Tavy's message.

"Yes, he gave me a message for you," he hesitated.

"Yes? What was that?" Sophia asked.

"He said that he would call on you later."

"Wonderful!" Sophia smiled and straightened Guillaume's petticoat.

Hiram and Abigail watched Rahzvon, who appeared to be notably disturbed with Sophia's exuberance with the message. They anticipated the inevitable rivalry, Abigail sharing Hiram's concern, even without having met the illusive sailor.

Rahzvon watched Sophia's dark eyes dancing with the thoughts of fooling Ian and Dirth, while chatting with Eloise. He sneered at the sight of the ring.

I have her uncle's approval. The sailor is in for a fight. Rahzvon walked over to Sophia.

"Sophia, I would like to speak with you...alone," Rahzvon said firmly.

Sophia smiled approvingly, "Certainly." She followed him to the hall. "Yes?" she asked, curiously.

Hiram and Abigail were engrossed in the interaction, with deep concern. Abigail stared to the archway wondering how Rahzvon would approach Sophia on the subject of Tavy. Hiram felt his pain.

Meanwhile, Rahzvon walked to the kitchen and stopped. Sophia followed. His intense stare, took Sophia aback.

"Rahzvon?" she asked nervously. He stood staring at her silently. "Are you still angry with me?"

Rahzvon did not respond.

In the parlor, Hiram checked his pocket-watch, noting that it was time to put their plan into action.

"Guillaume, take Hunter, he is two hands larger than Duff. You will appear smaller in the saddle, at a distance," Edward suggested.

"Very good, Edward," Hiram commented.

"In this condition, that is all I can offer. Call me the *idea man*," Edward said jokingly.

In the kitchen, Rahzvon stared at Sophia, taking her ringed hand in his.

"Did he give you this?"

"Who?"

"The sailor."

Sophia broke into laughter, but gained control immediately, seeing Rahzvon's adverse reaction. "No, my uncle Edward gave it to me. It is a 'welcome to the clan' gift."

Rahzvon turned away with embarrassment.

"Rahzvon, you are jealous of Tavy," she teased.

"I am not! I have no claim to you," he retaliated.

"Well then, perhaps you should," she said indignantly.

"Should what? Be jealous?" he scoffed.

"No, stake a claim."

"Then I shall. Sophia McDonnally, may I have permission to court you?" he said straight faced.

"You may."

Rahzvon stepped closer.

"*Leslew zaward skichared*, and do not forget it," he demanded sharply. I am going to get the horses." He saw Hiram standing near the doorway and walked by without comment.

Sophia stood at the kitchen window watching Rahzvon run to the barn.

"I shan't forget, I only wish that I knew what it meant," Sophia replied.

"I know." Hiram spoke without thinking.

"You know? What does it mean, Uncle?"

Hiram did not answer. *He is serious about this relationship.*

"Sophia, we shall discuss it later. I have to leave now, I expect you to 'hold down the fort' as your uncle Edward would say."

"But Uncle—"

"Not now, Sophia."

Sophia gave Hiram a hug, "Please be careful, I could not bear to lose you again. Could you please keep a special eye out for Rahzvon; he is very young and inexperienced?"

Hiram laughed, "Are we speaking of the same lad, the man who rescued me?"

"Uncle Hiram, this is a serious matter."

Hiram returned the hug and reassured her, "I know it is. He shall come safely back to you."

"Thank you, Uncle."

Chapter XVl

"Perfect Timing"

"Serene will be our days and bright,
And happy will our nature be,
When love is an unerring light,
And joy its own security."

—William Wordsworth

Hiram met Rahzvon in the barn. He placed the net in the Dugan cart and walked over to him.

"Your feelings for Sophia are stronger than I realized," Hiram mentioned casually.

"Perhaps, too strong, sir."

"Aye?"

"Not in the manner, you may believe, sir."

"Perhaps, you should expound on that statement."

"I doubt that you will comprehend this, but sometimes a man feels like he has stepped into a situation, that is more than he can handle." Hiram smiled in agreement and nodded.

"Mr. McDonnally, Phia is constantly challenging me. Sometimes, I question my judgment in seeking this relationship and at the same time, I am so drawn to her that I feel my life would be nothing without her. I never know what she is thinking from one moment to the next and—"

Hiram placed his arm over Rahzvon's shoulders, "Aye, vedriza mynoud tofmi?"

"Precisely."

"Son, welcome to manhood. Ours is not to question, *why?* Do yourself a favor, and do not try to understand Sophia and her unpredictable nature. I guarantee that you will lose many a night's sleep, pondering the inexplicable behavior of the opposite sex and it will be all for naught. Might I advise you?"

"I am always willing to listen, sir."

"I recommend that you respect the differences in her character. Enjoy the spontaneity in her decision. Naturally, you *will* attempt to defend your actions, for mistakes that you do not realize that you have made. But, a word of warning— it will appear that your defense has fallen on deaf ears, but remarkably, she will remember every word that you have ever spoken."

"If I might say, sir, life with Miss O'Leardon must be very interesting."

"Aye, and for that reason, I would not exchange places with any man. Now, we have their honor to defend, shall we go?"

"Thank you, sir," Rahzvon smiled.

"My pleasure."

Joseph Dugan arrived leading is mule just as they finished their discussion.

"Joseph!" Hiram greeted.

"Hello, Mr. Dugan." Rahzvon pulled back the canvas in the back of the cart.

"Good to see ye, Mr. McDonnally, Rahzvon, ol' Jock will be hitched up in a minute."

"Capital. Ready, Mr. Sierzik?" Hiram asked.

"Aye, captain."

Rahzvon and Hiram climbed in the back of the cart, safely hidden , beneath the tarp. Within the next few minutes, Joseph was driving them to the backside of the Duncan Ridge forest.

Guillaume, too, was moving swiftly towards Duncan Ridge and giving a very convincing performance as the young Sophia, well seated in the sidesaddle. He fought the coastal winds, which made their way inland, and thanked God for giving his mother the ingenuity to double-tie the bonnet strings. Several minutes later, he signaled Hunter to the right, off the road, and cautiously entered the field leading to the ridge. He spoke quietly, navigating the horse around the numerous holes and rocks scattered before them.

"Easy lad, mind your step."

Anticipating the possible need for a quick escape, Guillaume struggled to utilize his peripheral vision, hindered by the brim of the bonnet. He halted the horse to remedy the situation, reaching up to bend the annoying brim, which he found to be inflexible. *This is much too dangerous, my vision cannot be impaired! I am not about to meet my Maker wearing this outfit and carrying this.* He scowled down at the doll.

He moved Hunter to a nearby clump of trees, and began pulling on the bonnet strings to remove it. Guillaume kept a vigil watch, frantically fidgeting with the tie, which remained knotted. Finally, it loosened, just enough for him to pull the strings over his head. He withdrew the hat, lifted his skirt and swiftly removed his knife from his boot. He began chiseling erratically away at the brim.

"Confounded thing!" *The things I do for this family.*

Hunter began shifting with the rider's struggle to slice the fabric and keep a sporadic watch.

"Steady, I almost have it." Guillaume held the hat up for a brief inspection, and then replaced his knife and the remnants of the hat in his left boot. He pulled the tattered cap back over his head and slid the notably loose strings beneath his chin. "Much more efficient!"

"We wasted enough time, c'mon!" he instructed, guiding Hunter up the last stretch toward the hill above the clearing.

Joseph delivered Hiram and Rahzvon with the net, and returned to McDonnally Manor. They situated the net between two trees, relatively high, up over the path. Then they took their positions to watch and wait.

"Albert and Joseph should be posted with the constable in the ravine in the next few minutes." Hiram noted. "Both outlets to the Ridge are covered." Hiram suspected that Ian and or Dirth would watch "Sophia" make the drop and head either north to the highlands or south through the woods.

"I have to hand it to Edward for suggesting the idea of the net," Hiram remarked. "I guess his extensive reading of mysteries and westerns, has its advantages."

"Mr. McDonnally, do you honestly believe that we can succeed with this? The timing has to be perfect."

"If for any reason, our timing is less than accurate and we fail miserably with the net, we take him down with our bare hands." *He shan't terrorize Abigail or anyone else ever again.* "He is not leaving these woods alone," Hiram added with conviction.

"Yes, sir." Rahzvon nodded.

"Never doubt your abilities, son," Hiram said confidently. "We have very special young lady waiting for us. We cannot disappoint her. You would not want the sailor to have free rein would you?" Hiram smiled.

"No, sir," Rahzvon grinned, thinking 'great minds think alike'.

"Speaking of timing, I would wager that we should have seen some sign of them by now," Hiram looked disturbingly at his pocket watch.

Rahzvon surveyed the branches above him, "Hold on, I can possibly get a view of the clearing."

"No, we need you right where you are," Hiram insisted.

At the top of the hill, Guillaume made a final check for any sign of Ian and his accomplice.

Where are they? They are out there somewhere. Do not disappoint me, Hunter. Rahzvon may keep McTavish at bay, away from Sophia, but no one shall keep him from moving in on Allison, if I shan't make it back.

A sudden blast of air pulled the hat from Guillaume's head. His hand shot up to reposition it and hold it in place. *Capital! How am I to manage this?* He fumbled with the strings, unable to tighten them. Time was of the essence and he had no other choice but to dedicate one hand to the bonnet and pray that he could hold on with the other and release the doll without losing his seat.

Time for my coming out! Guillaume straightened in the saddle. "God be with us, give it your best go, boy!"

He took the only alternative and placed Charity's arm in his teeth, gave the horse a sharp kick and a snap of the reins. Hunter pulled out in full strength, cantering towards the boulder. Guillaume rocked smoothly with the stride with a tight grip on the reins, eyes keenly focused on the rock.

"What the—" Dirth watched in the distance as the feminine figure holding down the strange headpiece, pulled the doll from her mouth. *Spirited lassie.*

Considering the speed of the pass, Guillaume made the drop as daintily, as possible, and circled back. Without further delay, he encouraged Hunter to the road in a full gallop. Guillaume held on for dear life, traversing the potentially dangerous area at an accelerated rate until they arrived to the safety of the road's sure-footing. Guillaume caught his breath, reached down, and patted the heaving horse.

"Thank you, lad." Horse and rider moved at a relaxed steady pace to meet with the others.

The first phase of the plan was complete and Guillaume Zigmann rode proudly, despite his attire, to the ravine to report his success.

In the meantime, Hiram and Rahzvon were perched in the trees, barred from visual confirmation. They intended to rely on the sound of approaching hooves to alert them, but the northern winds whistling through the treetops were presenting a glitch in their plan.

"Sir?" Rahzvon called to Hiram.

Hiram did not respond.

"Sir!" Rahzvon elevated his voice.

"Aye?"

"How are we to hear them coming?"

"I fear we shan't. Be prepared, we may have to respond without warning."

Rahzvon gestured his confirmation. He peered down at the path below, experiencing a deja vous to his adventure with Sophia in the Grimwald woods. *Not to worry love, I will return. I am not about to let the likes of that sailor to comfort you, while you are grieving over me.*

Hiram repositioned himself in preparation to jump. He scanned the woods to the spot on the path where he had found Abigail sobbing, after Dirth's assault. He tightened his hold on the branches until his knuckles turned white. A look of torment swept across his face.

Ian appeared at the top of the ridge minutes after the drop. With the coast clear, he signaled to Dirth who shot out into the clearing toward the doll from a knoll below. To Dirth's surprise, Ian sped down from the ridge, snagging the doll, and headed directly for the woods.

Blasted traitor! Dirth thought and immediately doubled back to enter the woods from the south to cut off his deceitful partner. Anticipating this move, Ian cleverly entered the woods north edge, out of Dirth's view, did an about-face and made a quick exit for the road northward.

Dirth whipped his horse mercilessly, driving it down the path through the woods towards Hiram and Rahzvon's snare. Hiram and Rahzvon were drawn from their thoughts of the women by the sudden appearance of Dirth racing steadily toward them.

This is impossible! Hiram thought knowing they could not calculate the drop with the necessary accuracy.

Rahzvon looked to his mentor in a panic. *He is moving too fast!*

Hiram made the instant decision and signaled Rahzvon to drop the net, believing it would at least serve as a deterrent. Rahzvon hesitated with confusion.

What is he doing? Remembering Hiram's instruction, he acted accordingly and released his side of the net.

The large net dropped from the trees covering the path below, spooking Dirth's horse. Dirth fought to gain control, pulling on the reins and yelling as it reared.

During his distraction, Hiram cued his partner, "Now!" Dirth glanced up to see the men leaping from the trees and drew his knife in recognition of his attacker. *McDonnally?*

A second later, Hiram lunged at the rider, latching onto Dirth's clothes. With one powerful yank, Hiram pulled him down from the saddle, successfully dodging the swinging blade.

While the horse vocalized in retaliation and fled, Hiram clipped Dirth's leg knocking him off balance. Dirth landed hard on his back with a groan. In one swift movement Dirth's large form exploded back on to his feet cursing, "It is over, McDonnally!" He planted a swift kick sending Rahzvon crumpling to the ground and then came down hard on Hiram. The two wrestled to the ground with Dirth quickly gaining control.

Hiram's temper raged, as he lay pinned beneath the black clad enemy. Hiram's arm muscles were taut exerting every ounce of strength to restrain the blade, which the vile opponent pressed toward his throat. He clenched his teeth and held his own.

Dirth's demonic eyes and foul breath hovered over Hiram's, face. Dirth smirked, forcing the blade closer and threatened.

"No one stops me from gettin' what I be wantin', not MacGill, not even the grand Master McDonnally. The money and the fire-headed lassie will be mine."

Dirth's confident eyes flashed, unaware that the mere mention of Abigail provided newfound strength to his captive. Hiram's eyes burned with contempt. His grip on Dirth's wrists slowly inched the blade toward Dirth's fiendish grin.

"Never, again!" Hiram forced out the words. Dirth's eyes widened with the unexpected weight of Rahzvon on his back. Before he had time to retaliate, Rahzvon dropped the corner of the net over Dirth's head and pulled back. Dirth fought to remove it and maintain control of the master. Hiram seized the opportunity and knocked the knife from Dirth's grip while Rahzvon expertly bound the culprit, now covered in the net from head to toe.

Hiram stood up, flushed and exhausted, brushing the dust from his clothing. "Good work, Mr. Sierzik." He reached out and shook his hand.

Hiram picked up the dagger and turned it over several times. He stood, irate, breathing hard over his prey. The livid Master took one step closer. Rahzvon watched, his heart pounded, fearing that Hiram's hatred for Abigail's tormentor and his captors would tempt him to retaliate in the worst way.

Dirth's eyes were anxious with the victor's large frame luring over him and his boots only inches from his head.

"What are ye waitin' for McDonnally?"

Hiram looked down at his feet, then at Dirth's smug face, thinking, *I shan't dirty my boots on the likes of you. You are filth.*

Hiram stared pensively at the weapon tight in his hand. His lip snarled and his dark eyes narrowed. His grip tightened around the handle. Rahzvon stood silent, nervously waiting and watching, knowing that he should do anything necessary to prevent Hiram from making a grave mistake.

All rationale was on the verge of being lost to Hiram's need to strike back, when suddenly, a blinding light appeared on the blade and the sacred words of Hiram's grandmother, Sarah, redirected his thoughts.

Grandson, remember, "Bless them that curse you, do good to them that hate you, and pray for them which despitefully use you, and persecute you.

Hiram's tension slowly dissipated. The knife slipped from his hand to the ground. He spoke to Dirth in a controlled tone.

"The High Court may deal with you."

Rahzvon breathed a sigh of relief, with deep respect for his father's dear friend. Dirth, on the other hand, lying in the dirt, looked up and sneered. "Ye fool, ye coward."

Meanwhile, Albert and the law officers seized Ian MacGill en route northbound to the ravine. He put up a good fight, but was bound and on foot for the pleasant walk to the village jail.

Guillaume rode with one of the law officers to assist the team in the woods. In the clearing, he spotted Rahzvon motioning victoriously of their success. Alas, the two culprits were then escorted from the moors to a dismal future.

Eloise and Allison arrived shortly, driving the carriage to the top of the crest. They moved quickly down the ridge to the heroes in the clearing. Abigail poked her head out the door, when they arrived.

"Sir, are you lost?"

Hiram leaned on the door, staring up at her, "No, just enjoying the view," he smiled.

"You know, although the snakes have been chased out of Ireland— we have our fair share here in Scotland. Might we invite you to ride with us?"

"In that case, I think that my handsome, brave, friend and I shall accept your offer," Hiram smiled and winked at Sophia in the carriage.

Rahzvon and Hiram climbed in next to the very pleased women.

"Where are you headed, sir?" Abigail asked as she sat comfortably next to Hiram.

"To one of the most appreciated homes in all of Scotland," Hiram replied as the carriage headed through the hills.

"Are you referring to the large one where the congenial, freckle-faced Irishman will be arriving soon," Abigail grinned.

Hiram closed his hand around hers. "Aye, that is the one. I *had* planned to speak with him, but since I discovered that his pitiful sister refuses to eat leg of lamb, I may have to reconsider," Hiram said with absolute serious-ness.

Abigail's smile fell from her lips. She turned helplessly to Sophia.

"Aye, I may have to reconsider...altering my menu," Hiram teased. "What do you think Sophia?"

"I beg your pardon?" Sophia asked, confused.

"Do you think that a man should give up his lifestyle for a woman's love?"

Sophia smiled at the vagabond next to her, "Most assuredly."

Hiram turned to Abigail, "As my niece is known to have knowledge beyond her years, I shall have to take her advice and reconsider." He brought Abigail's hand to his lips and kissed it. Rahzvon's fingers, inching towards Sophia's, resting on the seat between them, did not escape Hiram's notice. Rahzvon froze, locking glares with the watchful uncle, until Hiram gave his nod of approval.

The foursome enjoyed animated conversation of the day's events and the visual entertainment of Guillaume trotting along side on the return to McDonnally Manor.

To everyone's delight, Edward was waiting in the portal waiting to greet the triumphant warriors. He followed them into the parlor, praising them for their victory and anxious to hear the details of the capture.

Several miles away, Beatrice MacKenzie sat on the porch swing of the Stewart home, lamenting her situation, when Mrs. Stewart appeared at the doorway with an envelope.

"Birdy, this came for ye yesterday when ye were walkin' in the garden. Sorry. I canna seem to remember a thing these days."

Beatrice took the envelope, "Thank you, Mrs. Stewart."

Beatrice returned to the swing and examined the correspondence. The handwriting was unfamiliar to her. She anxiously opened the envelope and began reading the following note.

> *My dearest Birdy,*
>
> *Although our association was brief, I feel the need to confess my sincere pleasure in spending those very special days with you.*
>
> *Nothing would please me more, than to pay you a visit in the very near future.*
>
> *Yours truly, Daniel*

Early the next morning, Edward and Hiram sat in the study discussing *Riders of the Purple Sage,* waiting for the women to appear from upstairs to join them for breakfast. Eloise left her table preparations in the dining room to answer a rap at the door. She passed Edward en route to join her, believing that there was a chance that Naomi had returned. Eloise opened the door and accepted a letter addressed to Naomi. The postman, Mr. Kilvert bid the housekeeper good day and continued on horseback to the Dugan cottage.

"Mr. McDonnally," Eloise asked Edward, "could you please give this to Naomi when she arrives? I have to go the cottage to fetch a jar of jam."

"Of course," Edward took the letter and examined it, discovering that it was posted from London. He held it for a moment, contemplating its contents, when his curiosity got the best of him. *It may be important. I am her husband, so to speak.* He wheeled into the parlor to the window, checked to see if he was truly alone, carefully opened the letter, and began reading.

> *Mrs. McDonnally,*
> *The young man of whom you inquired, when you were visiting London, returned to the shop this afternoon for some spools of thread. I nearly forgot to ask him about his mother. He said that her name is "Beatrice."*

Edward's jaw dropped. *Naomi's mother?* He continued reading.

> *He said, in retrospect, that he found it odd, at the time of your meeting, that you resembled his mother. Unfortunately, he reported that she has been missing this week past.*

I hope this clears up any confusion. He, too, is interested in contacting you, hoping that you may have information to her disappearance. He left the following contact information.

Edward quickly placed the letter in his inside jacket pocket.

Capital! Wheelchair or not, this wedding is going to be perfect! You, my love, are going to get the surprise of your life, I shall see to it! I will get Jorgensen, on it, directly.

In the study, Hiram had reviewed a couple monthly bills and was clearing away the correspondence from his desk, when Sophia bounded into the room.

"Good morning, my adventuresome niece."

"Good morning, Uncle Hiram. May I speak with you for a minute?"

"There is always a spare minute for you, love." Hiram sat down in the chair and swiveled toward her with his hands folded in his lap.

"Remember when we were in the kitchen and you said that you knew what Rahzvon had said to me?" Sophia asked.

"Aye."

"But first, I must ask you, Uncle, how is it that you are familiar with Rahzvon's native language?"

"I visited his country, years ago. In fact his father was a good friend of mine."

"His father, a friend of yours?" Sophia could not believe her ears. "Does Rahzvon know this?"

"Aye, we discussed the matter, that *night* in the barn."

"And he did not tell me?"

"Perhaps, he felt that the timing was not quite right, as yet." Hiram leaned back in his chair. Their dark McDonnally eyes met. "Yes, Sophia, I am very familiar with the language. It seems that *you*, too, are fluent."

Sophia stood trapped in his authoritative gaze, remembering that night in the barn. *Oh dear, what did I say to you?* An expression of sheer guilt fell across her face.

"Now, Uncle Hiram, in my defense, I must admit that I have no idea as to the translation as to what I said to you. It was something that I heard Rahzvon repeat several times that evening," Sophia said with contrition.

Hiram threw back his head and laughed until the tears rolled from his eyes. Sophia watched with shock.

"Sophia, you my dear, are priceless! I love you," he said wiping his eyes.

Although confused by his amusement, Sophia took advantage of his forgiving mood and asked, "Uncle Hiram, what *did* he say to me in the kitchen?"

Hiram noticed Rahzvon standing behind Sophia, in the doorway of the study. Hiram nodded to him.

"I think *that* is something that you should hear from the man, himself," Hiram resigned.

Sophia turned and Rahzvon offered his arm.

"Good day, Uncle Hiram."

"Good day, love."

Sophia, hopeful with the prospects, joined Rahzvon. Hiram overheard Sophia as the couple entered the hall. He shook his head to the familiar ring of her inquiry.

"You knew that my uncle knew your father and you did not tell me?" Sophia asked pointedly.

Rahzvon and Sophia left the mansion and crossed the drive to the privacy of the distant meadow. Hiram stood concealed at the window's edge observing his niece with her first beau.

The couple stopped amidst the swaying heather and faced one another. In seeing Rahzvon take Sophia into his arms, Hiram returned to the desk.

Rahzvon spoke with apparent difficulty.

"Phia, as you are aware, at this time, unlike some, I am not a wealthy man. Regretfully, I have no family, no property... no country. Although I am but a pauper, I *do* have an inheritance. I promise you, that someday, I shall return and reclaim it... for the present time I shall work very hard. If you had any doubts, please dismiss them, now. I am not a fortune hunter, Phia."

Sophia listened respectfully to his confession and gently confirmed, "I never doubted your integrity, Rahzvon."

He smiled slightly and continued, "Phia, do you believe that a man... a man of no means, could— could you find happiness with one who has not proven himself to be a worthy provider?" He held her hands and looked to the ring adorning her finger.

Sophia moved her hands to his shoulders.

"Rahzvon, up until these past months, I have lived most of my life in want of the material things in this world. My mother may have not had the means to provide the luxuries of life for me, but I never once considered her to be an 'unworthy provider', nor did I suffer severe discontentment in her care. I learned early on that happiness comes from within."

Sophia reached up and gently touched Rahzvon's face. "Do you not know that I would sacrifice all of this of which I am entitled, to be with you?"

Rahzvon held Sophia close and whispered down to her with desperation, "Phia, my feelings for you are like none other than I have *ever* experienced. I cannot lose them, nor can I lose you... I have lost everyone and everything that I loved. Do you understand?"

Tears streamed down Sophia's cheeks.

Hiram sat facing the window, with a sense of hope and peace.

Tell her son, Leslew zaward skichared,
"we shall walk as one, through eternity."

"Enjoy the Spring of Love and Youth,
To some good angel leave the rest;
For times will teach thee soon the truth
There are no birds in last year's nest."

—Henry W. Longfellow

Non-fictional facts referenced in Threaded Needles

*Rahzvon's homeland and native language are fictional products of the author's imagination

Percheron and Hannoverian Horses
Manchester
Zane Grey's novel *Riders of the Purple Sage*
Popularity of pinochle card games
Red-throated Divers
Joseph Highmore – English painter
Oxford
Train collision at Armagh
Machrie Moore Stone
Joe Jeannette- world famous boxer
Sara Bernhardt's Legion of Honor Award
William Shakespeare
"corrie"- kettle
Red fox
Red deer
Herman Melville's *Moby Dick*
Kate Cranston's tearooms
Deeside, River Dee
Jordanhill College of Education
Pine martins
Ellisland-Robert Burns' farm
Edinburgh rock- candy sticks
Gigot- leg of lamb
Isle of Lewis-guga delicacy
Stonewall property divisions
Norwich
Story of Jeanie Wheaton
 (story of author's mother)
High Court

Poetry Excerpts from the Chapters

Acknowledgements

Agneta Inga-Maj Garpesjo-Davis
Swedish Language Assistant

Chronicle of the 20th Century.
New York: Chronicle Publications, 1987

Grun, Bernard. The Timetables of History: A Horizontal Linkage of People and Events.
New York: Simon and Schuster, 1982.

Illustrated Encyclopedia of Scotland.
Anacortes,: Oyster Press, 2004.

Kidd, Dorothy. To See Ourselves. Edinburgh: HarperCollins, 1992

Lacayo, Richard & Russell, George. Eyewitness 150 Years of Journalism. New York: Time Inc. Magazine Company, 1995.

Summers, Gilbert. Exploring Rural Scotland.
Lincolnwood: Passport Books, 1996

Webster's International Encyclopedia. Naples: Trident Press International, 1996.

Webster's New Biographical Dictionary.
Springfield: Merriam-Webster Inc, 1988.

*I am a firm believer
that education should be an ongoing endeavor.
I stand by the unwritten law
that education should be entertaining
for young and old alike.
Thus, I incorporate
historic places, people and events
in my novels
for your learning pleasure.*

*With loving thoughts,
Arianna Snow*

TO ORDER

*Patience, My Dear,
My Magic Square,
Spring Spirit
Threaded Needles*

Visit: www.ariannaghnovels.com

Watch for the fifth in the series!